Victims
of Circumstance

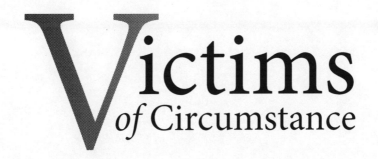

Victims
of Circumstance

KENNETH JOHNSON

Contents

Getting My Feet Wet. 11

Saturday Six-Thirty Pm...15

Rose..16

Dominoes Falling 21

A New Life, New Beginnings 24

Two Thousand Eight, 9:50 P.m...26

A Black Knight In A Red Car 28

Dreams..37

Day One 44

Day Ten 45

Six Months…..60

My Parents House. 62

June 23… 64

June 24..65

Seven Pm.. 66

My Brother Russell 72

Meet And Greet 79

One Week Before The Wedding..86

Wedding Bells 89

Living, Loving, Snag 93

Several Months Later...95

Another Day In Creston Lake 96

Two Years Married 99

Three Years Married 104

On The Other Side Of Town 108

Mink.. 112

A Minute Later 115

Simple Plan..116

One Hour Later 125

Questions And Answers 128

Good News, Bad News 136

A Mother's Love.. 144

It's A New Day 147

Work To Forget 151

Date Night 158
Black Angels 160
A Righteous End 163
A Family Affair 166

Epilogue 169

I'd like to thank Pam who was always in my corner and the catalyst to my completing this book.

Also, I cannot forget my sons Kenney II and Kenndel who are great writer themselves and have given me the inspiration to follow through.

Our lives are ruled by circumstances and becoming a victim at some point is inevitable. How we choose to handle it is up to us except when it is out of our control.

…GETTING MY FEET WET…

WALKING TOWARDS THE subway, I was fearful of being consumed by the humidity that threatened to suck the life out of me but the expected belief of it being cool underground was foolish. Talk about jumping out of the frying pan into the fire, above ground was a hot eighty-five degrees and here below had to top the hundred-degree mark. On the platform were all of New York's necessary pain in the ass tourists and for the tenth time I promised myself to stop being lazy and put my old Honda in the shop to avoid public transportation on the weekends. They were all around me, huddled in their individual groups speaking little to no English. It was funny to me that it seems there is this secret understanding that when in New York there is safety in numbers. Our reputation throughout the world precedes us yet they keep on coming. Sometimes I wonder what they say to friends back home about entering a dark, hot, rat infested tunnel that looks far too dangerous for humans.

"DAMN, Where's the fucking air? I looked around for a cosigner to my small outburst but no one dared show any interest to a crazy man. I leaned forward close to the edge of the platform to see if any train lights were headed down the track. A small outburst signaled the sighting of a subway rat as he skittered by catching my attention but nothing more. The rats knew their place and I knew mine so neither had to worry about ever being fearful of the other.

-Hallelujah," twin beams of headlights lit the sides of the walls, growing brighter by the second, the racket of metal wheels screeching on metal tracks deafening to anyone else except a native New Yorker. It was an anticipated sound, always bringing a small fraction of joy to the person waiting on its arrival. As the cars sped by, I like many others peeked in the windows of the slowing train searching for the best place to be positioned. When the doors opened the rush was on to locate a vacant seat with minimal contact of another passenger. I made a break for my preferred spot, the empty two seater at the end of the car. After the victory of claiming a seat, it was time to settle down for the long ride to my station.

Earlier, I was engaged in a must win tournament against three competing dojos. I say must because it felt like my vanity was at stake. This was not my first match and I had the trophies to prove it, but it was by far the most important to me. On Pop's suggestion of finding a hobby away from the house, I joined the dojo of the Camouflaged Tiger when I was sixteen. Mama's guilt about Russell compelled her to smother me as the remedy to his failure. She cooked, cleaned, and stayed in my business in and out of school, one being the questioning of female friends on what their intentions were with me. For my sake, Mama was avoided at all costs, something Pop had taken notice of. Seeing the direction we were headed, he tried talking to Mama, tell her she was overcompensating but she was adamant so here I am. My love for this sport was immediate. The first day, I showed up in a white gee and a Jet Li mindset. Our sensei who preferred to be called Mr. Hu, insisted that meditation is key to being a great martial artist. Our bodies needed to be free from the negative signals our brains will send us while we train. I'm sixteen and the last thing I wanted to hear was meditation and deep relaxation techniques. For the first three months we sat in a darkened room, learning to be one with ourselves. First day of the fourth month all that meditative practice was put to the test with Mr. Hu dictating our every move. Every fifteen minutes a command was shouted out.

-STAND, in unison we stood on one leg, arms extending back and forth, hands in prayer position. (Dropout, dropout). I fell more than I stood.

-BEND, feet together, palms on floor, fingers outstretched, thumbs touching. (Dropout, dropout), My back, my stomach, my head, I'm going minute by minute now.

-SQUAT, arms in front then to the side constantly rotating. Icy hot suited me better than meditation but I persevered. (Dropout, dropout, lots of dropouts). From one stretch exercise to the next we practiced with constant repetition of well-scripted moves producing swollen parts I did not know existed besides the expected hands and feet. Talk of giving up became my new mantra of every new day.

Mr. Hu, ever observant asked,

"You become drop out too?" Embarrassment and the thought of Mama back at home would be a greater pain.

"No Mr. Hu, I'm no dropout."

"Good, more practice, lots more practice." I couldn't begin to say how long it took for me to master these techniques, but my steady progress albeit slow, motivated me to work harder with Mr. Hu who, with no sympathy, constantly added more difficult techniques. The more experienced guys practiced with the grace of a bird of prey never thinking about their next move, always allowing their reflexes to keep them out of harms way. It was a level of expertise I dreamed of but now was unsure of ever reaching. The next phase of training just about finished off the remaining few beginners.

There came a time when Mr. Hu pronounced me ready to spar with my colleagues. Talk about happy, until being knocked down so often the dark blue mat we sparred on was renamed Brian's mat in my honor. Again doubts resurfaced about picking the wrong hobby weighed heavy on my mind. We had started with forty and one year later we were down to three, then two. In the street there was no problem with me holding it down but in here, they all were my superior and the standing rule was to test me at any time on my offensive and defensive skills. One day in particular, if not for common sense after getting my ass kicked good during a brutal match against three opponents, a real fight would have broken out so I left. It was summer, school was out and to avoid seeing Pop, I hung out in the streets hoping later than sooner he would find out. My friends saw Pop first as he walked up the street towards us and gave me the heads up. The thought of running came to mind but not in front of friends, especially the girls so putting on a tough façade was the next best choice. Pop being a street man would understand what my pretense was all about and play along until we were alone. Pop ignored my friends, standing in my space as if it was just the two of us.

"I didn't raise any quitters. Russell never quit, he may have messed up but he didn't quit. You are paid up for the rest of the year, finish what you started."

Many setbacks later and in my third year I fought in my first amateur match against the dojo of the dancing sidewinders. Here, I met my archenemy, the one person that beating became a top priority. His mouth was mighty and I'll be damned if he couldn't back it up. This was also his first match but you wouldn't know it by his antics. When it was time for us to fight, he stared me down while beating his chest, pointing at me then the floor. It was a pitiful imitation of the master, Muhammad Ali to get into his opponents head. It worked for him, you it won't, I thought. Shutting him down was a given, to prove as I had proven to guys like him that talk does nothing but get you a harder ass whipping. The ref cried begin and we charged at each other like two male lions competing for the pride, winner takes all. A quick sidestep and two hits in the side mixed with a knee that I couldn't defend, sent me to the mat.

"POINT, Jeremy Tompkins." Okay, he has some skills so now I'll show mine. We touched hands.

"Fight," the ref announced.

"Whoo-hoo strike one, get ready for strike two," he said patting his stomach and pointing at my leg.

"Yea well, It's my turn." I went on the offensive with a double kick to the chest then the head. It was a fast maneuver, designed to catch the opponent off guard and take him down. Something went wrong because I found myself on the mat again. He had swept my foot from under me and pushed. I sat there for a second listening to POINT, Jeremy Tompkins being called by the ref. At four of my eight count I stood up.

"You okay," the ref asked.

"Yea, yea, I'm fine."

"How many fingers am I holding up?"

"Three." This nut was on the opposite side of the mat acting a fool. Okay, he got to me.

"I'm about to send you home," he said. We fought for another minute or so before the clock ran out with me taking a lost on points. All said and done, I had gotten my butt kicked and disrespected at the same time. To further shame the dojo and myself, I hurled curses in his direction seeking to regain some dignity. Mr. Hu grabbed my arm and whispered in my ear.

"Student you are not ready. His disrespect is your distraction and it means nothing when skills are involved. You must meditate more." Iron Foot, the moniker that fool's peers gave him, went on to receive a second place trophy while I was banned by Mr. Hu from participating in the next tournament. We would meet again in two state championships and one city tournament that year and that damn foot always managed to end my victory run. Last time he broke my ankle with an illegal kick, which cost him a point and me the match. His smirk said it all yet still he opened his mouth.

"Yo man, I'm going to give you some advice, find something else to do."

"Good fight, next time I'll be more worthy of your skills," I said, with Mr. Hu standing by my side.

"Next time? Next time I'm gonna knock your lame ass out." At home with a cast, I acted like a spoiled kid for the better part of two weeks complaining to anyone who would listen. Pop had heard enough and although he was a man of very few words he had some for me this day.

"Son you need to stop bitching and deal with the problem, it damn sure won't be your last. History has shown that in the midst of adversity you will either try harder or try less, so which are you going to do.

"What! I started laughing. When did you take up philosophy, Pop?"

"Bottom line knucklehead, do you want me to help you get past this?"

"Yea, I guess so."

"I'll take that to mean yes Pop, please and thank you. I'll see you in the morning and I suggest you get some rest." When Pop closed the door my complaining began again but this time it had to do with what I had just gotten myself into. My father was the guru of workouts. If I survive him, Iron foot can forget about taking home a first place trophy if he has to fight me for it. That thought alone made the upcoming torture of Pop's workouts bearable. He had me mornings and evenings and the dojo for three hours in the afternoon. My mornings, five a.m. no less, consisted of grass drills and running. Grass drills are variations of exercises mixed together to work more than one part of the body at a time. Repetition speed is also built into it making it one of the most hated but the best workouts your body will love after it gets over all the pain first. In the evening we spent our time at the gym where I worked the speed and body bags.

Saturday six-thirty pm

IT'S BEEN A tough year and a half since our last encounter but I was ready for the one who seemed to have a permanent claim on my first place trophy. The showdown was to take place at the Jacob Javits Center in Manhattan. I arrived early to meditate, aligning myself with my surroundings, something like what the Chinese call Chi. Weapons hung from the ceiling beams giving it that gladiator type of impression along with the poster sized pictures of famous martial artists and their various movies displayed mainly to capture the younger audience's imagination. The popularity in martial arts had resurfaced in the last two years due to an outbreak of a younger more aggressive version of thugs on the streets. Result: more Dojo's, more competition and bigger audiences of curious onlookers trying to decide if they or their child should become part of the culture. A newly admitted dojo named 'Tribe of Great Strength' was making a strong run for the state championship title also. I didn't want to lose sight that winning consistently was necessary in order to meet my rival or he me. A loud clamor arose on the other side of the divider, whistles blowing, drums banging, whooping and hollering all this to indicate Iron foot's entry. He was a confident son of a bitch, if nothing else.

"WINNER, JEREMEY TOMPKINS," the ref announced as my match began. An involuntary glance in his direction earned me an embarrassing wink from the bastard.

"BEGIN," the ref announced.

"KILL HIM SON!" Oh Yeah, I invited Mama for the first time to one of my matches, something I had never done before and I don't think I will ever do again.

…ROSE…

S HE LIVED THE life of a child for nine years before a chain of events beyond her control made it necessary to put childish behavior aside. By the time of her fourteenth birthday the transition into foster care was complete. If that was all to the story she might have been able to recoup her youth and however painful at first, move on. Unfortunately, this was a case of survival of the fittest and Rose had decided. Rose's mother, Pearl was fifteen when she gave birth and on arrival from the hospital found a packed suitcase in front of a locked door with an address. That stop lasted nine years in a shelter for homeless teens. Now twenty-four Pearl had to make room for other teen moms. She was Section eighted to a small two bedroom walkup on Sutphin Blvd. in Queens. Rose remembered it well because while in class a bewildered counselor noted that her mother had signed out minutes earlier and left for their new home. She was taken to the Administration office while the counselor caught up with Pearl at the bus stop.

"Aren't you forgetting someone," the counselor asked between exhausted breaths fresh from a run.

"Who, Rose? She belongs to you now."

"No Rose, no money, that's the way this system works."

"Oh, well then let's go get my baby." She tucked her arm under his, babbling about nothing as though this mistake could happen to anybody. This was a warning largely ignored because of facility overcrowding. Pearl smiled as she apologized to her daughter with the excuse of wanting to make sure the place was in order first before coming back for her.

The apartment above the Chinese restaurant consisted of a matching white plastic couch and love seat combo that had seen better days left from the previous tenants and a small table that bore the carvings of gang signs on every visible inch of its surface. This made up the entire décor of the front room. The bedrooms followed the same nondescript pattern with Pearl taking no interest in adding anything to change the room's dreary appearance. What was there was all she needed, a bed and a dresser to take care of business, nothing more. Sheets taken from the shelter made perfect curtains once nailed to the window frame. Rose was delighted to have her own private bedroom and she got busy adorning her walls with drawings and pictures of her favorite stars. Pearl on the other hand had to become the independent mother she never wanted to be. It didn't take long before her depression fueled the need to escape reality, which transitioned into the use of narcotics. Beauty ran in the family and Pearl put hers to good use in order to feed an increasingly insatiable habit.

It was ten p.m. on a school night when Rose finished her homework and went to bed. Pearl had been entertaining most of the day and needed a pick me up. She promised the last visitor an extra ten minutes on his time if he could wait while she made a quick run. While waiting, nature sent him to use the bathroom but in his haste he opened the door to Rose's room instead. Recognition of his mistake was immediate but he didn't close the door, at least not right away. Normally, a thirteen year old asleep in panties would not garner a second glance but this one was an exception. As his eyes adjusted with the help of a stream of extraneous light filtering in from behind him, the sight of this young flower with a body that rivaled Pearl's was amazing. Half of her light pink panties disappeared into the butt crack, exposing a basketball sized, blemish free cheek. His right hand held onto the growing protrusion in his pants while his imagination went on a roller coaster ride of lust. She stirred, frightening him as she seeked comfort in a different position. He closed the door partway so as not to be noticed but when no scream followed, he opened it back to another sight better than the first. Rose, now on her back had managed to twist her worn hand me down pajama top in such a way as to show one breast in all its glory. Goddamn, what a sight, he thought, thankful for the extreme temperature of the apartment. He wrestled with the idea of touching those large breasts as they heaved ever so slight in synchronous rhythm to the beat of her heart but decided it would be safer to be an observer. On the street below the window a car horn blared, Pearl came in the house and Rose screamed as she pulled the covers up over her. He backed out amid apologies but never took his eyes off of young Rose. She could hear her mother calling him all kinds of perverts as she screamed for him to get out, then sudden silence. Wondering what could have happened, Pearl calmed Rose's fears when she entered the room asking if everything was okay. Rose assured her mother the man had not touched her as Pearl sat down on the bed.

"You're turning into a beautiful young woman, she started. You look like your father, the bastard. When we met he was in his early thirties, tall, dark and handsome. I mean he had that GQ look going on. Nice car, money and the need for a fine young woman by his side to complete the perfect package, which as luck would have it, was me. The man promised we would always be together and like a fool I believed him. You know, you have his big beautiful eyes and dark complexion. Stand up and let me look at you. Damn girl, when did you get that body? Shit, I didn't get mine until I was fourteen and then, well, soon after that you popped up. Anyway, your looks are the best of both of us, which makes you a hot commodity."

"Hot commodity?"

"Don't play dumb with me girl. You see these men coming and going all day and night. It's my best assets that I use to make us some money so we can eat. Let me ask you, are you still a virgin and be honest, I won't get mad if you're not. Shit, with that ass alone, I know all them horny little boys are begging everyday."

"Yes momma, I'm still a virgin."

"That's good girl. Look, Momma put her arm around Rose's neck pulling her in close like they were about to have a sisterly talk. There's a man on the other side of that door that wants to help me out with the bills. He liked what he saw when he came in here and asked if you were available. I told him, hell no you ain't nothing but a baby, but goddamn Rose if you don't look all of twenty. You sure you still a virgin?"

"Yes momma, I'm positive and I want to stay that way."

"Okay, okay, Momma wanted to be sure she heard right. Oh, I didn't tell you the good part. Mr. Smith, that's the man in the other room, offered me one hundred dollars if you could do one tiny, little thing. Think of it as a favor to me." Rose was young but she was far from ignorant. She had seen enough in her young life to know that the only thing a strange man would want from her is sex, but she could be wrong.

"I don't know Momma. What are you asking me to do?"

"Just make him feel good sweetheart. It's real easy, Momma will show you. Her momma searched her face for some sign of acceptance. It took a minute for Rose to comprehend the full scope of the statement but when she did, the thought of being a party to such a vile activity visibly shook her to the core. Undaunted by the negative reaction, Pearl continued with the belief of talking her into them becoming a team. I'll do most of the work making sure he's all worked up until he's about ready to pop and all you have to do is get him off with a couple of licks, no more than two minutes I promise and guess what, you're still a virgin. Just do this for me and who knows, you might like it enough to become my second best asset. She nudged her daughter as she joked. We'll be rich and move out of this shithole into a real fancy place crosstown. Rose with eyes shut tight blocked out Pearls voice with her hands as she shook her head wildly from side to side. Pearl could see that her argument on the benefits they would have if they shared in the prostitution business was not working. She stopped talking and stood up, disgusted.

-Ungrateful little bitch, she spouted with her lips formed into a downward curl. I'm on my back all day and night trying to take care of you and here you can't do one little favor. That little bit of change they give me for taking care of your ass ain't enough for shit. Now, thanks to you I got to humiliate myself so we can eat tonight.

The pillow hushed the pitiful pleadings of her mother as she begged for a chance at earning the hundred dollars. Mr. Smith informed her she was worth the twenty he had originally planned to pay and not a penny more. Pearl got down on hands and knees and hiked her butt high.

-I'll bet some of this virgin ass is worth that bill."

"Bet, let's get busy but work on your daughter and there will be twice as much in it for you."

"Don't worry, Pearl answered, as she led him towards the bedroom, I'll have that little bitch in line next time for you. But right now, her hand stretched to receive the money, you are in for a fuck you will never forget."

Soon the only sounds to be heard were the familiar thump, thump, thump of sex along with a moan thrown in here and there. Rose stayed huddled in the corner of the tiny bedroom afraid for what the future held.

Word had spread after that about the hidden gem in apartment four. Every low life, rapist, con man, wannabe pimp, and opportunist paid for Momma's time. The sight of a beautiful young virgin living amongst the scum was to them an oasis waiting to be exploited. On any given day there were at least two men waiting on the pretense of seeing Pearl but wanting a glimpse or moreover to be first in deflowering the beautiful daughter. Rose stayed trapped in her bedroom seldom sleeping always guarding the broken door that now leaned against the opening, having been kicked off its hinges a month ago. Some of the men traded stories of their near encounters with the beautiful girl and decided teamwork would be the best way to get at her. Mr. Smith, whose real name was Jimmy, and Mr. Smith, Trey waited until Mr. Smith, Rick went in with Pearl. Jimmy eased into Rose's bedroom followed by Trey.

"Goddamn, I didn't know she was this fine, I want to be first, Trey said in an overly excited whisper."

"Hell no, I won the flip."

"Fuck the flip."

"What?"

"Nothin', forget it, Come on, and hurry up."

"Shut the hell up before you mess everything up." Jimmy stripped from the waist down and climbed on top of the sleeping Rose, at the same time going for the wrists. Rose was at once awake, the dreaded moment here at last catching her unawares. She could just make out the semi naked man on top and heart-thumping terror gripped the young girl as her mouth readied to scream. Trey seized the opportunity to ram a gag down her throat. The plan, keep her quiet, hold her tight, one get on, get in then the next. The element of surprise and the fact they outweighed Rose by over two hundred pounds, aided in their assertion that the rape will go like clockwork. Rick was doing his part making noises in the other room like he was the bitch about to have an orgasm. The pair had come up with extra cash for extended services to keep Pearl busy as long as possible. The men knew they would have to be fast, a little taste for each, bust that cherry, destroy her pride and turn her out. If they were lucky, a little mother, daughter action down the line, but that was a thought for another day.

Dominoes Falling

"FUCK," TREY YELPED, snatching a bloody hand from between sharp teeth. A wild swing caught Jimmy in the face, knocking him off balance. With a second gained, a knife was retrieved from its place under the pillow.

Faint fiery looking streaks of steel flashed its intentions in wide arcs emanating from the sharp six-inch blade Rose wielded as she slashed at any moving target. Amid long piercing screams, she bucked and kicked as Jimmy fought a losing battle to regain control, red marks appearing on his arms bearing proof of this. Total mass confusion ensued in the dark room with Jimmy colliding into Trey as they both went towards the door after he jumped off Rose. Neither could see well enough to pinpoint the location of where next the blade would strike so in a mad life or death dash, the entangled would be rapists tumbled out onto the living room floor at Pearls feet.

"Money or rape charges, you choose." They paid her extra protesting all the way out the door. She glanced in to ensure Rose wasn't dead and called next. Rose sat cross-legged on the bed, holding onto herself, shaking like a leaf on a windy day. She felt sorry for herself and prayed death would sneak up and end this miserable existence. Luck or the grace of god saved her today but what about tomorrow? There were no assurances for every day of the week for no telling how long. Her only small reprieve out of the bedroom to the bathroom or kitchen was while momma slept. Other than that, every day a man was in that other room and every day there was a problem with at least one of them. The surprise squeezes, the nasty remarks aimed at her, more close calls, the man standing right over her with his huge thing in his hand sliding it up and down its length with this look she couldn't describe as nothing but crazy. She had awakened and screamed but he paid her no mind, instead continuing to touch whatever body part he could get his grimy hands on. At the time Pearl was too busy with a threesome to check on her and the man didn't stop until gooey liquid squirted out the tip of his penis all over her. The man displayed a toothless smile, thanked her for the show, turned and walked out of the room. It went on and on with the inevitable looming in front of her.

Rose turned on the lights and spotted the pretty girl with the tear stained face and upside down smile looking back at her. In a fit of helplessness, her mind screamed fuck this, fuck men, fuck you and you and you and especially you, Pearl James. The defiant statement strong in its utterance, drifted away on invisible wisps of compassion for that girl in the mirror. Curious, she now studied that girl, seeing in her for the first time a beautiful, intelligent young woman. The help she had been seeking stared back followed by that moment of extreme clarity, like the turning on of a light bulb but a hundred times more brilliant. Her resolve came quickly as did the complete change in personality. The dicing up of Trey and Jimmy didn't make major news but the neighborhood grapevine was thick with the juicy gossip.

"Man you heard what happened the other day. That pretty ass girl in apt four lost her mind and stabbed up the place. I think she killed Trey and Jimmy."

"Nah man, I saw Trey right after it happened. He said the little bitch was high as a motherfucker, probably got into that crack shit her mama's doin'. She scratched Jimmy but they took the knife from her and got freebies from mom."

"I knew something had to be wrong with the girl, her momma just as fucked up as could be. Good lookin' piece of ass though."

Instead of staying away the stories brought more men to Pearl's to see the pretty girl gone mad. Rose heard about some of the gossip being spread and decided to give them their money's worth. She was making her bathroom run one evening and spotted Jimmy sitting in the middle of two men on the couch. The dirty bandages on both arms were a testament, he was the one in her room that night one month prior.

"Hi sweetie, she said" ignoring the other men surprised looks as she went into the bathroom.

Ten minutes later Rose sashayed pass the gaping mouths of all three wrapped in a short bath towel showing bare wet fourteen year old flesh from her feet to her thighs. Before she went into her bedroom she looked back at Jimmy.

"I know you, she said in her sexiest voice possible for a youngster. You the man came in my room a month ago. If you still want some of this virgin pussy you better come on and no need to close the door, I'm sure your good looking friends want to see the fucking you gonna put on me." Jimmy didn't move nor say anything not knowing what to make of her offer.

"Hey sweetheart, I'm willing to help you out of that cherry situation," one of the men said.

"Another time baby, I want the brave sexy man who had the balls to try and take what he wanted. She blew him a kiss. I'll be waiting.

"Is that the bitch you said was crazy? Man you better get your ass in there and tear that pussy up. Jimmy had to take Rose up on her offer but when he got to the door, Rose whipped a Taser from behind her back and shot a spike into Jimmy's chest knocking him backwards a good two yards. He convulsed at the feet of the two surprised friends who knew it was time to get the hell out of there.

Rose yanked the pins out of him, thanked him for coming and returned to the bedroom. Pearl opened her door to see Jimmy laid out on the floor moaning. Not knowing what else to do, she rolled and kicked at him until he was on the other side of the door, which she closed and locked. Rose was leaning against the wall when Pearl turned around.

"YOU GOT TO GET THE FUCK OUT OF MY APARTMENT, YOU LITTLE BITCH, fucking up my business."

"I ain't going nowhere, but I bet you are."

"Where do you think I'm going, who did you call." It took one week for the bitter standoff between mother and child to end with a visit from a child abuse counselor. She arrived at the height of a loud argument where mother and daughter stooped so low as to exchange punches between each other. Pearl found herself being arrested for a host of charges and Rose was made to leave for emergency placement in foster care.

...A NEW LIFE,
NEW BEGINNINGS...

THEY LIVED ON tree lined Sycamore Street on the Upper East Side in a beautiful brick home. The neighborhood was graffiti free with clean sidewalks amid flowered gardens on manicured lawns. The refreshing scenic change gave Rose a sense of release from the guarded alter ego existence forced on her. Once inside, the smell of some good home cooking was the first aroma to hit her nose. Once she and her mother had left the shelter breakfast, lunch and dinner became fast food. They headed into the back of the house where the scent of fresh flowers replaced the first smell as her new foster mother introduced the other four foster girls whom she was drawn to at once. They got along well and after a month had passed Rose settled into the routine of school, chores, and being a girl. One night Mr. parker, her foster father, waited until the house was sleep, before entering Rose's room to complain about his wife's inability to have sex. She listened not knowing what else to do until he decided she would be a workable substitute for the night. The pitiful approach changed to pleading while at the same time taking advantage of her. Young Rose was no match for him. He used brute strength to rip away the flimsy material and hold Rose down with a hand clamped around her neck. While she was busy trying to breath her virginity was taken in one painful push. He talked as he forced himself on her about how they will work out well together and he didn't know she was a virgin but now that he was the first he was going to teach her all he knew about sex. He droned on while Rose lay there in a daze unable to believe all the shit she went through to prevent this very thing from happening. She ran away that night only to be picked up by police the next morning and soon after was placed in a different home which in a matter of days she was again attacked in her sleep.

By the age of eighteen Rose had lived on the street for four years. Seething contempt gnawed at her until she resolved to seek revenge of both rapes. Mr. Parker always left the basement window unlocked. She went into the kitchen, grabbed a knife and tiptoed to the bedroom. There he was, at peace with himself with his wife snuggled up beside him. In one insane moment Rose ran at her rapist ex-foster father, raised the knife and quickly brought it down somewhere in the vicinity of his crotch as he lay sleeping next to his disbelieving wife. Two stabs and Rose ran out of the bedroom, and out the front door. His saving grace was having a cover over his body. His genital area was missed but the two superficial wounds close by got the point across. Young Rose stood fixated behind a car a short distance away watching the sudden burst of action as it unfolded. The rapist's wife was screaming bloody murder with all the antics of a class B actress as she spoke to the 911 operators.

"Should' a stabbed your ass too bitch, that would've given you something to scream about." She walked away with the expectation of being picked up sooner or later. Days passed with no signs of police because unbeknownst to her, Mr. Parker used an elaborate excuse for his injury and none of it had Rose's name in it.

Her second foster father was taken care of as he got into his car. A sawed off pipe made short work of his jaw and most of his front teeth. A note stuffed into his mouth read, (to my rapist, from you know who). This payment of retribution was fulfilled for two hundred dollars, money she earned as a waitress. At the police station the two men in question stood in a line up cheesing it up at the one-way window daring their target to ID them. A negative answer prompted the question about the strange note left in his mouth and once again the victim's answer was I don't know. By this time police had drawn their own conclusions leading to a release of both suspects.

With an address that changed daily, life was about what to eat and where to sleep that's safe. Alcohol became her elixir of choice, something to dull the pain of being sad and to help get her through the day. Her view on men was to use and abuse just as she had been. If a page were to be taken out of a Rose X book it would say, 'Keep your wits about you. Give nothing and take everything for survival is only for the strongest.'

A hard interior shell surrounded her heart to keep any emotional feeling toward a man locked away never to let him have the upper hand. Real men wandered into her life from time to time with good intentions but they too were met with a blunt coldness so extreme they sometimes feared for their own safety. It was natural for a man to be drawn to a pretty girl but to Rose there was always an underlying reason behind the help, still a few insisted on trying to get next to her which insured them a costly experience if not a painful one.

Two Thousand eight, 9:50 p.m.

"FUCK," SHE WHISPERED under her breath. Rose hurried across the street, stopping for a moment to respond to greetings from some of the regulars that frequented the Grass Roots Bar and Grill. The red light district where this and many other establishments set up shop were tucked away in a remote section of the city away from the well-travelled paths of the tourists the city counts on for fifty per cent of its economy. A mandatory bright red neon sign warned folks of the type of activities that went on inside. Blue collar crossed paths with white collar, their interests united in the pursuit of sexual gratification from the under aged models that worked at the clubs. On any given night one might see an elected official right up to the police commissioner himself, slinking around in a vain attempt at not being noticed. This was ordered a safe zone as long as the bar owner's private security forces kept the violence down to a minimum. The bar itself was a dive of a place patronized by lonely single men looking for one nighters, but cheaters, ass holes and any deviant who had five dollars in their pocket was welcome as long as he behaved. If you were looking for love, this was one of those wrong places they talk about in songs. She was supposed to meet Cross no later than nine-thirty to pick up money owed her for doing him a favor. He was still there, standing with his backpack on talking to some strange woman. His female partner had already taken over behind the bar and gave a 'what's up' sign. Rose waved back and pointed at the woman. His partner shrugged her ignorance and moved on to a customer. Poor Cross she thought, he's too nice to tell the bitch he's off duty and don't want to hear anymore of that woe is me shit. If it was another man Rose would have hesitated but a gay man talking to a strange woman, no sparks there.

"Hey Baby, Rose greeted as she sidled up to the handsome bartender pinching him on the ass. Glad I caught you in time for my money honey," she said as her hand came up. Cross hugged her warmly as he dug in his pockets and paid his debt. With a kiss on the cheek he hurried out the door forgetting the other woman he was talking to. Pockets full, Rose sat down and ordered a drink. At the far side of the bar next to the pool tables, stood the bouncer eyeing the new woman waiting for his turn to have a go at her. The waitress placed a drink at the table the moment she sat down specifying who the sender was. Without so much as a glance in the general direction of the bouncer she downed the liquor plus the next three all without the slightest knowledge of who sent them. As he was about to claim his prize, she stood up on wobbly legs still pissed but thanks to all the freebies she now had the courage to voice her opinion. His lips curved into a smile thinking that his new piece was coming to him instead. Rose felt a hard tap on her shoulder. She popped off of her seat and stood to face whoever had the nerve to touch her.

"You know that was rude what you did."

"First bitch, you ever put your hands on me again, my being rude is the last thing you're gonna have a problem with, and besides, who the fuck are you."

"I'm not a bitch but a little hood rat like you wouldn't know the difference. The woman's head recoiled at the sudden slap from Rose. Before she regained her senses Rose slapped her again this time putting everything she had into it. The woman went down to her knees, holding on to the stool for a crutch. The bouncer went into action as he rushed to the woman's aid. He hit Rose with a backhand as he knelt down and asked the woman if she was okay. A barely audible yea escaped her swelling lips as he helped her up with a stray hand getting a quick feel. He sat her at the table and turned his attention to Rose who was just now recovering from his hit. He snatched her by the neck and dragged her kicking and screaming to the door.

"Get the lady another drink and don't worry, she won't bother you no more." He used Rose's body to open the door and flung her into the street. The sudden thud of a young woman hitting the pavement startled the numerous partiers out looking for fun. Men were ready to come to the aid of the pretty woman that a man dared to hit but at the sight of the giant who tossed her, they figured it was best to mind their own business. Rose who would never ask a man for help in the first place, bounced up off the ground and jumped on the bouncer as he made his way back inside. She bit down hard on his neck, insistent on repaying the pain he caused her, except on a man six four, two ninety this was the equivalent of a pesky mosquito bite. A body slam against the building dislodged the poor woman from her hold allowing him to launch her limp body about eight feet into a cushion of spectators who pushed her away, so scared of drawing the crazy giants attention toward themselves.

...A BLACK KNIGHT
IN A RED CAR...

T HE CAR SKIDDED to a stop in the middle of the street startling those nearby at the scant inches it came to bumping into them. A well-dressed man jumped out, ignoring the cries of anger about the car's near miss and stepped in the middle of Rose's assault.

"Only pussies fight women, he said. Are you a pussy or would you like to try your luck on a man." He was impeccable in his blue Armani attire, which didn't seem to matter except for the shirt he removed as he spoke. The bouncer not the least bit impressed grinned. A buzz of voices went through the crowd at the interesting soon to be exciting turn of events.

"Turn around, walk away and I'll pretend like you were never as stupid as you look." The man known to his friends as Pop did not reply. He studied the big man, his years of street fighting helping to process what he observed. There was an art to fighting and Pop was considered a master. Chemistry and science mixed with practice and conditioning made him undefeatable for the ten years he'd been involved.

"You ready to do this," Pop asked. The bouncer eyed the little man who in any other mans eyes was not so small. It was a forgone conclusion in his mind that the pretty red car Pop got out of will be his reward after the ass whipping he was about to put on him. He'll take that pretty young bitch he spent his money on home in it and after fucking her, he might call his boys and let them have a go. The bouncer made a brief scan for the woman from inside the bar, not wanting her to leave in the five minutes this new fight was going to take. Mama told this story a hundred times and still she never tired of it. No one ever learned the man's name so Mama always called him Peacock, you know like the male bird trying to look good for the female bird. So Peacock turns real fast and swings, thinking he's going to get the drop on Pop. Pop's head jerked back as Peacock's massive fist breezed past, missing by fractions of an inch. A phantom return punch with enough power to shift the position of Peacock's nose while still into his missed swing amazed the audience. He stumbled back out of the line of fire to feel the mushy lump that was left, acknowledging the lucky punch he received. There was no pain but the busted vessels could not hold back the river of blood as it began making its way down his canal dropping onto the pavement. He held his head back while pinching his nostrils until the flow subsided, ignoring Pop who stood patient watching his every move. A few drops of red liquid stained his white tee shirt in honor of drawing first blood. Rose screamed out, "MY TURN" as she dragged her way to him. Without losing sight of his opponent, Pop scooped her up and out of the way. Fallouts from every club and bar up and down the street formed a wide semi circle as the recognition of a good fight spread. The avenue was littered with empty cars of onlookers who stopped to get a view of the action. Reflections of leaping lights seemed more alive as they bounced about with restless energy highlighting the makeshift ring from atop awnings meant to lure customers into their respective premises. Bets were placed, with Peacock still the favorite solely because of size. Spraying blood on an ever growing crowd with a strong snort hinted he was ready. Some agreed with the bouncer on luck playing a factor and alluded to foolishness for Pop not finishing it when he had the chance. Pop stood five eleven, two hundred thirty pounds of hard muscle. A one sided fight from the average mans point of view. How could Peacock have known he'd been beaten the moment he was sized up. Pop, by the way was just getting warmed up when Peacock renewed his attack with a vengeance. Enraged at a stranger doing what has never been done before, his bruised ego needed to be restored which raised his adrenaline level to achieve the necessary results. With Pop, it was all a matter of lessons taught and lessons learned. This is a wounded bull charging with no real direction in his actions. He is seeking a quick knockout in answer to his obvious embarrassment. Rose stood as best as she could right at the front cheering Pop on. This was the first time anybody ever stood up for her and this complete stranger was taking on the biggest man Rose had ever seen. Pop stood rigid as peacock lunged, allowing the speed of the big man to help flip him head over heels and land on his back followed by a quick but effective jab on closed lips forcing them to be ripped open from their owner's sharp yellow teeth searing their way through pink flesh. It happened so fast, if you blinked as some observers did, only the bloody aftermath was witnessed. Up off the ground in an instant, wild eyes pivoted around trying to determine the next move.

Everything up to this moment was timed and initiated to the letter. Pop could have ended it any time he chose but there was a lesson to be taught and

Pop was a damn good teacher. Again he waited with the lively crowd around him getting restless because things weren't progressing as they should. This was no knock down, drag out old fashion blood and gut spilling honest to god fight, this was a pro against a punk. People feeling cheated had the nerve to utter their belief in the unspoken sin of it being a rigged fight. Still they stayed, riveted to their spot as a paying customer would, knowing that one punch could turn their losing bet into a win. Peacock started at Pop again, looking more like a rabid dog in the midst of mind altering insanity, snarling and spitting as he went after his prey. He had had enough of this shit and now it was his turn to do some damage. Both men were about to answer their audience's cries to see more. Wild swings ripped the air apart in an attempt at landing something on the man in front of him ducking and dodging but always a step ahead. With the speed of a cheetah and the skill of a hungry shark, Pop blocked a right to his head to get in close. He started slow allowing for the force of the punches to be felt then picked up the speed to induce a rippling effect on the surface of peacock's stomach. In a last ditch attempt at stopping the onslaught, Peacock locked him into a tight bear hug with all intentions of breaking his back. The loud crack of two bone to bone head butts would make the stoniest of men cringe at hearing this but it succeeded in Peacock letting Pop out of his grasp. From a sideways kneeling position, Pop kicked and broke Peacock's kneecap. The scream of agony sounded like that of a demon being sent back to hell. Peacock was through, Pop was not. With a determined expression, he kneeled next to him and with slow, methodical patience worked his face over. Left punch under the left eye, left punch to the cheek, right punch to the nose, left, right, left, right to the lips, to the nose, back to the mouth. Blood covered older cuts as they poured from the new ones. His right blood engorged eye blew up like a balloon closing it completely, the left headed in the same direction. Rose trembled at the sight of such devastation and if this wasn't enough Pop now went back to work on the body. Every time Peacock attempted to protect himself Pop hit him harder. By the time it was over, Peacock had more broken ribs added to the kneecap problem, not to mention an innumerable amount of unknown damage. He now had a face only a mother could love if she was able to recognize him as one of her own. Amid a cheering crowd Pop put Rose in his car and whisked her to the hospital. He paid the bill, left her some money and wished her well. All this was done with no mention of compensation of any type. Rose knew she had found a real man and refused to stay without Pop there so he spent the night into the next day with her. When she woke up, he was sitting in a chair sleep. She got up and hugged him vowing to never leave his side. Six months later they were married and nine months after that Rose became Mama for the first time.

Those first years before me Mama drank too much, smoked a pack a day and still fought. The difference now was when Pop said enough, like the turn of a spigot it stopped. If Pop had to jump in a fight, that meant the other person was crazier than Mama, otherwise he'd just squash it between the two. As far back as I could remember my parents went out most weekends to the neighborhood bars together. Whenever they got home Mama was drunk and complaining while being carried by Pop. Never once seen him drunk though. When Mama went out alone as she did often enough, If you were ever blinded by her beauty and disrespectful like so many were, you ran a good chance on meeting Chan. Chan was the name she affectionately gave her seven inch Saigon blade. The knife was popular in the seventies because of the ease in which with a simple flick of the wrist the blade was out and locked, ready to do some damage. Pop had bought the knife years before he met Mama. It was kept as a memento of all the fights he and that blade had been involved in. While teaching Rose how to use it, Pop insisted how important it was to take care of such an instrument. He noted that a lot of permanent artwork was walking around out there compliments of the artist. Rose learned to have that blade switched out of its sheath before any offensive move could be made against her. Afterwards Pop gave it to her for protection whenever he was not around and she felt the need to go on one of her binges.

Once a man in a bar called her a bitch and she slapped the taste out of him. The man slapped Mama back and before Pop could come back from the bathroom good, the man was lying on the floor bleeding from a deep cut in the side. Suddenly liquor was always in the house so Mama wouldn't have to go out for a drink. Mama got drunk and went out anyway. You can't keep a born and bred street girl cooped up. Mama liked the streets and that was that. Anyway, you know Pop loved her because he always had her back, and who else would put up with all the shit through the years. Don't get me wrong, Mama would do anything for her man and she proved it many times over. In a strange way those two made for a perfect couple. When it came to being a mother, when she wasn't drinking, Mama was involved, you know, as a parent. Most of my single parent friends wished they received half of the attention I did minus the school visits. We were in the schoolyard one time and my mother showed up. A sampled version of some oldie came on the radio we were listening to and my mother broke out in a dance.

"This used to be my jam," she shouted. I was embarrassed as hell but all my friends loved her. Mama's hugs and kisses eventually earned me the nickname of Mama's boy around some of the kids at school. I laughed at the thought because in reality, that was the last thing I was. Mama chased after me while I constantly tried to avoid her but that didn't stop the jokes. Pop said I should be a little more tolerant of her because she was afraid of losing me like she lost Russell to the streets. I told him I'd try but as a kid the one person you don't want cramping your style is your mom.

Iron foot sauntered over and sat next to her with a shitty grin on his smug face. I ignored him and instead eyed my opponent in front of me.

"Hope you're ready," I whispered when we bowed. When the ref swung his arm down my opponent struck out first and I blocked. The succession of attacks and blocks repeated themselves until I made one purposeful switch in my routine and with practiced speed hit him with an open palm just under his sternum so hard he couldn't stand straight. A few more added shots sent him to the mat. His stance at the end of the eight count suggested a person in pain. At the drop of the ref's hand he backed away, taking up a defensive role trying to anticipate my next move. With the taste of victory on my tongue, I switched to a type of boxing style, taught to me by Pop. He blocked the intentional slow jabs and rights easy enough until my last jab lured him into a block allowing for a shot to the side of the face. The only thing stopping me from knocking him out completely was the protective headgear we had to wear. He felt the repercussions of that blow as indicated by his sprawled figure on the floor. The ref grabbed my arm and announced,

"WINNER BY A KNOCKOUT, BRIAN MARSHALL!" I looked over towards Mama eager to gloat in Iron foot's face but he was gone. Mama was jumping up and down though. I put on this fantastic show and he had the nerve to leave early.

The matches were now history with me taking two first place trophies and a first place medal. Tired but happy we celebrated over drinks afterwards. I'm looking forward to a hot bath and some sleep before calling Pop in the morning and bragging about myself. My unwinding began when I felt the cool air blowing in the train car stifling the muggy feeling of the hot summer evening. I thought back to some of the nights craziest moments, especially with my off the wall mother.

"HONORABLE REF, ARE YOU BLIND? THAT WAS A FOUL. The ref gave Mama a look and turned back to the match. OH HELL NO, I KNOW YOU DIDN'T GIVE ME THAT SHUT THE HELL UP LOOK. BRIAN, YOU SEE WHAT HE DID?" I took an eight count and at the refs' allowance, went over to Mama.

"Mama, please calm down. As my guest if you disrupt the match it will cost me a point. Don't worry about the ref, I got this."

"All right, she said lowering her voice, I'll do it for you son but he better watch his attitude. I will not be disrespected by anybody especially a youngster."

"Mama, he wasn't disrespecting you." Mama grunted as she sat down and promised me again she would behave. At the signal to fight my concentration was off due to my mother's antics and I got caught by a flurry of punches knocking me off balance just enough to receive a surprise roundhouse to the side of my head. Thanks to Pop's intense training I was quick enough to partially deflect his kick but I still hit the mat with a loud thud. My opponent nodded his approval and Mama jumped out of her seat again.

"WHAT THE HELL!" she spat, hell bent on fighting my opponent herself. I smiled at the sight in my head. The pissed off ref announced one point for the knockdown and one point for bad sportsmanship on the part of my mother.

"MA, you have to sit down so I can concentrate and try to win a medal for you. Mama slapped her hand to her mouth but it was too late. The ref wanted her removed and quite frankly so did everyone else. I hurried up and escorted her outside to a waiting area giving her a kiss and continued with the match. It took everything I had to comeback and win within the allotted time frame eventually coming in first. Mama, you something else." Sleep came at me with a vengeance, something I couldn't fight off.

They got on at the far end of the car and all heads turned with mine following suit, my drowsiness replaced with curiosity. I remembered hearing there was a runway show taking place somewhere in the center. These five stood out with their unique style of daring attire meant to capture the imagination of what men desired. Their mini dresses showed off physical attributes of varying degrees enhanced from many rigorous workouts in the gym. One young lady's top was cut so low, if she had to bend down for any reason, her large breasts would surely spill out for the pleasure of her captive male audience. Attention also was given to the friend's dark, hard nipples pushing against flimsy see through material begging to be noticed. Silver, gold and platinum jewelry hung from their designated places jingling or shining with the slightest movements of their bodies.

A passenger who blocked some of my view got off at the next stop and there she sat. How could I have missed the finest woman of the bunch when they entered? My glances were many but I ached to get up and stand nearer to them for a closer look but that would have been too obvious. An eleven on a ten chart, my intense examination revealed no flaws of any kind to be seen on her baby smooth cocoa brown skin. Ruby red lips clashed with the bluish tint of hair in a way that neither over shadowed the other. I expected loud with a touch of embarrassing ghetto drama, something that would subtract their appeal to give me a sense that I wasn't missing a thing. I was happy to be wrong about these women who exuded grace and self-assurance because now I like my counterparts dreamed of my arms wrapped around any one of them. Without warning she stood up after a quick scan of the car, I guess to make sure there were no available seats. The short mini she wore was the same dark chocolate color as her skin with etchings of red lace around the hemline. With shameless pleasure I allowed my gaze to rest on her legs and follow a path upwards where her thick thighs began to show themselves. The view was abruptly cut off, forcing me to add my own flavor to my imagination. The eloquent way her long slim manicured hands moved when expressing a thought and that raucous laugh showed she was by no means inhibited. The friends didn't seem to compare to my girl, although I could easily imagine myself in their beds as well. My stomach churned when I thought my somewhat stalker like behavior had been discovered after her eyes boldly connected to mine for the instant it took to complete her observation. Paying me no mind, she turns away and they continue conversing while a young woman with child sits in the vacated seat. Now I get a full look at her rear and see that eleven was the correct rating but what of her mental aptitude. Only a shallow man could tolerate a dumb pretty woman for any extent of time but from my vantage point she appeared to be intelligent and fun to be around. Sure this woman was already taken, I wondered as to the type of man that drew her to him. Handsome, rich, a woman of that caliber would not be remotely interested in someone like me, average at best. Anyway, I didn't have the wardrobe or the money to wine and dine on that level, another good reason not to be bothered. I will stick to my dreams and enjoy her presence as long as it lasted.

She took out a piece of paper and borrowed a pen from the one male in the group. I hadn't noticed him among all that beauty but I am impressed with his success at getting her number. Damn, if I could be the fly on her shoulder just to know what he said. I laughed, if I was a fly on her shoulder I wouldn't be paying him no mind, instead I'd be trying to get a peek at those perfect looking breasts sitting up there on her chest in that without a doubt braless top. Sad to say, her train stop arrived with her taking a fast walk the length of the car towards me and dropping that same yellow piece of paper on my lap. With a wink she disappeared into the crowd. Surprised and ashamed all at the same time, I quickly stuffed the note in my pocket, unwilling to read it with all her friends still riding and no doubt watching to see what I would do. I never looked back in that direction again, instead feigning sleep until my stop came up. When I opened my eyes they were gone. The note read-

"Hey shy guy call me-347-654-3020."

By the time I got home the note had burned a hole in my pocket same as a hundred dollar bill would. This woman with no name who could probably get any man she set her eyes on asked me to call her. Why me and why in the hell would she play a dangerous game like giving her number to a stranger. Something tells me I'm on the butt end of someone's fucked up sense of humor which with a jump shot of the crumpled up paper straight into the garbage on my way to the bathroom, I did not want to be a part of. Everything was forgotten when the small beads of hot water started bouncing off of my embattled body. Bruises dotted my arms and legs in a bluish black hue the result of the tournament fights and Iron foot in particular. For a few minutes I felt rejuvenated as I reminisced once again.

"Fight!" the ref announced as a loud uproar sounded from my teammates. All eyes were trained on Iron foot and me since we were the last fight of the night. It was known throughout the martial arts world that we thought very little of one another. He was a smartass, one of the traits I hate most in a person. Knocking his perennial silly ass grin with all of those immature comments right down his throat is what my dreams consisted of. Our match was broken up into three parts. Armed combat covered two parts with the weapons of our choosing and unarmed combat completed the third part and scored the highest. In life the chances of getting into a conflict with a weapon are very slim. It is your hands you will always have access to as weapons, therefore it is seen as the most important. The ref monitors the fight but the title rested on the shoulders of three judges with each match being the best three of five. Iron foot took the offensive hoping for an early score using his foot to strike out towards me with three fast kicks in an attempt to knock me down. I spun on him and returned with a kick to his thigh he felt but didn't do any damage. As the match wore on Iron foot reminded me why I had to beat him. He attempted the same illegal kick that broke my foot before. The foolish move was avoided but he received the obligatory one warning. I could feel the heat in my stomach and the fever on my head as I unleashed a flurry of punches and kicks to his midsection then to his face and back to his body yet again. He blocked some but I was able to score several times. This match as far as I was concerned could only be won one of two ways, knock out or a technical knockout. Points meant nothing except for teaching purposes. I tried to gauge what state of weakness he was in but all I saw was that damn grin.

"If that's all you got then you will not win this fight fool." His iron foot came out of nowhere and the next thing I knew the ref was making sure I could continue the match. During my standing eight count, Iron foot eyed me from across the mat. Suddenly he put his hands to his head mimicking me with a headache. The crowd laughed,

"FIGHT," the ref announced after I nodded my okay.

"Don't flop out on me yet, sport, I want to practice on you some more," he whispered on his approach and received a kick to the midsection, which sent him down on the mat. I stood over him goading him to get up, something that wasn't my norm earning a warning from the ref and being ordered to the opposite corner. Iron foot jumped up and down hitting his stomach to show he was ready. We traded front kicks, back kicks, hits to pressure point areas, all the lessons taught and practiced to near perfection. He caught my kick and with a twist of his wrist he spun me off balance and on my stomach. Before his finishing attack to score the point I turned on my back and kicked him in his chest to jump back on my feet. He was good, as a matter of fact very good, which would make my victory that much sweeter. I circled, never losing sight of his position watching his hands moving, preparing for an attack. Steeling myself, my focus is to counter unless, a misstep. A feint to the head followed by a left cross and a foot sweep and Iron foot went down where he is finished off with a kick in the chest. He got up, a smile spreading across his lips until my lips turned up a smile mocking him. I think he knew this wasn't the same guy he'd been beating for so long. Too bad for him he was right, when he was told to give it all he had. Mama who was let back in had the crowd on their feet chanting my name. Cautious apprehension replaced his once cavalier attitude. He got caught in the side of the face with a lunging backhand snapping his head back while I went into a boxing stance. I blocked a right, ducked under his left cross and hammered him with a left to the mid section following that with an elbow to the back of the head when he bent over. It was a medium hit, just enough to give him notice. He went down on one knee and the ref pointed me to the opposite corner. He came at me slow at first with a shuffle of his feet was to begin his patented move, one foot high the other low and he on his hands. It was beautifully choreographed and two years prior probably would've cost me the championship. A step back with a return kick sent him sprawling to the mat.

"You lose," I announced after the eight count was finished.

"WINNER BY KNOCKOUT, BRIAN MARSHALL." Mama jumped up,

"THAT'S MY SON WHO WHIPPED THAT ASS." She danced around not paying any mind to the alarmed looks of the spectators. Mr. Hu whispered in my ear, still not ready, but I see what you're up against." So much for sportsman like respect.

Newly refreshed I entered into my bedroom ready and willing to let the sandman take this round. As sleep claimed me my mind drifted back to that mysterious black woman who owned the number in my garbage.

...DREAMS...

HUNDREDS OF MEN stood in line holding lottery tickets, each checking their numbers to see if they won the prize. The same beautiful woman from the train is waiting on a cloud for the right man to rise up to her. No one has the winning ticket and they are all staring at me standing there with my empty pockets turned inside out. I realize I have the number one ticket but it's in the garbage can that's on fire. Rolling out of bed on three hours sleep, the balled up paper with the mystery woman's number on it found its way back in my hand. What if this wasn't a bet? With no hesitation phone numbers were pushed for the sake of knowing the truth. The butterflies were taking over my stomach by the fifth ring, one away from my decided hang up point when a female's sleepy voice answered.

"Yes, this is Risha, she said."

"Wow, a beautiful name for a beautiful woman."

"Hmmm, eight thirty in the morning and the perfect line to not get cursed out, I could get to like you."

"I apologize for the early wakeup call but I couldn't sleep until we spoke. By the way my name is Brian."

"Well Brian, I guess I was wrong about the shyness."

"Not necessarily, we would never have this call if you hadn't taken the first leap of faith."

"Well-spoken Brian, so far it seems I picked a gem but the jury is still deliberating over you."

"May I ask you a question?"

"Straight to the point, you just keep getting better, go ahead ask away."

"I am dying to know, why did you give me your number?"

"I could say it was charm and sex appeal but we both know I'd be lying. I saw you salivating over in that corner and I thought it was kinda' cute the way you kept looking away so I wouldn't notice. Almost couldn't keep little man in your pants, huh."

"It ain't that little."

"Uh oh, I'm scared of you. The guy you saw with us had been sniffing at me all night at the club. We were celebrating my new career path and he figured if he could put enough drinks in me he'd get a fucking good night. I insisted he include my friends, which after all was said and done, set him back a thousand dollars and still no closer to the bedroom. The poor fool was so desperate he left his car and followed us to the train station begging all the way. By the time we got there he figured that sex from any of us would be all win-win. We wanted to see how far he would go so we got off at different stops to see what he was going to do." A man after my own heart, I thought.

"It took everything in me not to laugh when I borrowed his pen. I can only imagine what his face looked like when I said good bye and gave you the note."

"Then I should be grateful to him."

"Well, I guess you should at that." Before we continue this further, where may I ask were you coming from at that time of morning for me to be so lucky to run into you on that train? Not a girlfriend's, I hope?"

"Let's just say you were the completion of a very good night for me."

"Very good night, Hmm, Still doesn't answer my question. Where is this going to lead us Brian?"

"I was coming from an important martial arts tournament from which I took first in three events. My buddies and I had celebrated just before you saw me."

"OOOH, a karate man, Are you like Bruce Lee?" I laughed out loud.

"No not quite, I answered. First off Bruce Lee was a Kung Fu master and I am a Kung Fu student."

"If you received all those trophies, I'm thinking you are more than a student. I wouldn't mind being 'your' student." Shivers went through me at the sound of that one.

"I'm sure that can be arranged."

We lapsed into a marathon of conversation. At one point during our question and answer period no subject was taboo. Scary, kinky, interesting but most of all revealing. We were like children, embarrassing each other and yet learning the things we wanted to know and being just plain nosy. It was fun listening to Risha squirm as I had when I was on the hot seat. She was more down to earth than I would've thought from someone as beautiful as she. I was a typical man letting looks dictate what the personality should be like but I was learning. Hour after hour passed until we needed to take a bathroom break, with cell phones still glued to our ears in the bathroom. For a minute Risha got real quiet,

"Risha, RISHA?"

"Yes, I'm here."

"What happened," I asked.

"Giggle, Man, can't a woman have a moment. Let's say a lot more happened than just pee."

"Heh, Heh, so you feel better now."

"Yea but now I'm hungry. What time is it?"

"It's twelve o'clock."

"Noon? You know Brian, I usually don't let anybody keep me away from my sleep for too long so I think one good turn deserves another, don't you agree."

"Yea I guess, what you have in mind?"

"A poem."

"Any particular artist in mind?"

"Make something up."

"You and me we're in this thing…"

"Damn, that was pretty good. You jumped on that so quick it sounded like you were prepared."

"Thank-you, I aim to please." I was surprised at myself at how this strange woman could make me do things I never thought I would do. She was the one.

"I'm not going to lie, I get good vibes from you Brian as you can probably tell so I'm thinking, let's go on a date. If you're anything like you are over the phone, you might get lucky. I think you should accommodate my wish, agree?"

"Hell yea, give me a time and a place."

"Wow, It's been a minute, huh."

"Sorry, yea let me check my calendar and get back to you, say, in a week.

"Three PM, the Manor Hotel, inside there's a bar named Logans. My company owns the building so say my name and where you're headed and you shouldn't have any trouble, funny man."

"The Manor? I'm impressed. What is it you said you do again?"

"Didn't say. Just bring your cute ass to the hotel."

Two thirty found me sitting in Logans and signaling to the pretty waitress who worked the tables. The place was cozy and dimly lit offering intimate appeal for couples wandering down from their rooms with the need for public display in a private setting. The opposite side was comprised of bigger tables for larger groups but it still maintained the ambience of coziness. The walls were filled with physical artifacts of every type of sport played in the world. An authentic Mickey Mantle famous number seven jersey owned a spot above my head. How many of the damn things had he worn in his career? Every sports bar across the nation had one, like BB Kings, Lucille held the same position in a musical theme. Risha appeared at the entranceway at three on the nose scanning the few patrons looking for me. I waited for her to notice me as I drank in every bit of her as she stood there. Seeing me, she pointed, then clapped her hands in silent appreciation as she floated on air to my table, or so it appeared to me. I took my place beside her pulled chair, playing the role of a gentleman.

Before hello, hi, how are you, good to see you, she sealed our lips together, parting them solely for the entrance of her tongue. Now that's my type of hello.

"Had to get that out the way, she said as she took her seat. Risha waved her hand for Sandy's attention. The cute waitress had earlier gone out on a limb and whose number I now held in my pocket. Could I have a rum and coke with a twist of lime, and refresh his drink." Risha sat down across from me and looked me up and down.

"Are you satisfied?"

"Well your luck is still holding out if that's what you mean. You received a B minus on the kiss exam. But we still have other tests to run. What's your appeal without clothes?"

-Ha, Ha, I'm joking, don't mind me. What about you, how you feeling, lucky right?"

"Am I that transparent?" Sandy delivered our drinks, serving Risha's behind her back so I could receive an all men are dogs frown from her, following a perfect rip up my number mime. Chalk it up to male ego.

"The train, remember?"

"Riiight, the train." We settled down for an enjoyable evening finding out more about each other. Sometime during our conversations a huge plate of chicken wings appeared and for some reason those were the best wings I've ever tasted.

"You know Brian, You're easy to talk to, smart and witty. Why in the hell hasn't some pretty young woman snatched you up yet? Risha tapped her long slender brown finger lightly against her lips. What is it you're hiding that I should watch out for? Are you a woman in disguise? No Risha, she answered to herself out loud as she kept up her gaze on me. Is he a pervert, I hope so to a point. A wicked smile crossed her lips. I got it! You have a super huge ding a ling that scares women off. Is that it Mr. Brian, should I be afraid of what's lying dormant until the time to strike?" Raw, funny, and uninhibited, I like this woman.

"A little, I answered back as the laughter rolled out of us. It's been so long I might hurt you with my comeback. Seriously though, I'm just an overly hard working man that never takes the time needed to find a woman."

"Jesus, I thought I worked too much. Well, I'll change if you change."

"I'm working on it as we speak."

"Brian, I have a question? The unconscious readjustment of her posture relayed the seriousness of what she had on her mind.

-Tell me, what kind of relationship would you like this to be?"

"What kind? Well, I really didn't give it that much thought." I felt like I was transported into a boardroom meeting where my answers might well determine my future.

"I'm waiting, Risha replied, her hands folded on table. Lead with light humor, build up the ego a bit and BAM hit me with the business at hand. In the mini seconds that followed, I attempted to read her facial expression to get a feeling of what type of answer to give her. A blank yet placid look is what I got along with the make up your mind already impression when she leaned back and crossed her arms. I did not want to hesitate because that would show I'm trying to put my best foot forward instead of being real. Friends with benefits would do for starters, I thought but I said,

"We can start by being friends."

"That's what we wasted all this time for, friendship.

-Is that your final answer?" she asked with mock intensity.

"Well Yes, NO, I don't know! Shit, I'm only trying to tell you what you want to hear." I took the best foot forward approach and panicked when it backfired. My underarms got damp as my hopes of being with this beautiful woman was slowly fading away. Risha took my hands sending my neurons into a frenzy. With a steely stare, she made it crystal clear of how she felt.

"Friends I have plenty of and no desire to fuck any of them. I'd rather since we're so busy spend a moment in time between us then go our separate ways."

"Honestly, that moment in time sounds good but I'd prefer to stay around if you don't mind." A smile spread across her pretty face. I think I got it right.

"Go on, I understand the first part but explain the second part?"

"I would like you to be my woman, okay."

"Okay."

"Okay?"

"Sure, I'll be your woman."

"Great. That was easy."

"Didn't look like it from where I sat."

"Whatever. So what's next?"

"Am I going to be the man or the woman in this relationship?"

"You're the woman, so let's get out of here."

"Where?"

"Anywhere, how about a ride around town. I need to get to know you better, my way."

"Mmm, now that's a good idea."

"I'll call a taxi."

"No, you get the check." Risha pulled out her cellphone and a moment later we were at the lobby door of the hotel.

"You like?" she indicated as the gray Limo pulled up to the curb.

"Hell yeah, that's much better than what I had in mind." As the car pulled off from the curb we kissed with the intentions of seeing who will fall first in the lust game.

"I see you've been holding back." Risha pursed her mouth as she snapped her fingers.

"Only my man receives the full package as you can see. All others get to look and dream, and maybe a small sample from time to time depending on my mood."

"Well, since I'm now your man, I intend to collect on that dream and no more samples."

"Excuse me, but where are we headed?" The drivers voice over the intercom surprised me. Risha spoke up.

"We want to take in some sights Dale, whatever you find interesting."

"So you want once or twice around the block?" Risha giggled,

"I think a few more miles added will do just fine, thank you."

"What's up with your driver, he sounds like an asshole and how do you know his name?"

"Oh don't mind Dale, he likes to joke a lot. Trust me if you stay around long enough he will grow on you."

"Well one thing I plan to do is stay around. Now where were we?" At the press of a button a secret compartment flipped around revealing wine, cognac and brandy together with four glasses.

"We were toasting."

"Ah, Castel Del Monte, 1950, a very good year indeed but my pallet calls for something how shall I say, can go straight to the head." Risha laughed, snatching the bottle from me.

"This Castel del Monte has a cure date of last year. 1950 is when the company was founded, silly man."

"Oh, so we definitely not drinking that. My vote's for the cognac and you my dear?"

"I concur, my dear."

"Good, any nays?" Dales hand slowly went up.

-What, not you Dale, you drive. This damn intercom was on the whole time?"

"Sorry, it's off now."

"Turn it back on for a second. Dale, the first toast is to you, the greatest driver in the world. Now, any nays?" Dale held a thumbs up.

"Motion passed, let the celebration begin. I flipped the intercom off while Risha led with the second toast.

Four drinks later, Risha handed me her empty glass and collapsed into the soft plush leather seat allowing it to suck her into its web of comfort. As for me one more toast to the good fortune of being on that late train when she got on. The toast ended with an interesting view of my Risha's short dress not being able to do its job properly for need of comfort, diverting my attention to smooth, caramel colored legs, reminding me of what I hungered for. Taking my chances thanks to an alcohol fueled burst of lust, my hand settled on a bare knee while her neck and face were showered with kisses so slight, they would be a secret thrill for me alone. So lost was I in quenching my appetite, hearing the almost inaudible moans escaping from her lips was a surprise and a sure sign of a mission headed to success. Confidence overflowing, my hand slid to her inner thigh to begin a search and discover mission up slightly parted legs. Soft and smooth as I had imagined, it was a major test of will power to take it slow and enjoy every distinct mind blowing touch.

My tongue met her tongue to begin a battle, neither backing down always searching for a way around the other. My hand continued its journey unimpeded, happy in the diversion the war of tongues caused. My inner thigh massage paused to receive special compensation in the way of a stray hand that had found its way to rest on an erection threatening to rip through my pants. Her arousal triggers an involuntary impulse compelling her legs to open further as an open invitation of surrender. I reach my destination but only for a second due to Risha bolting upright, shutting down the path to her luscious valley before I could realize my fantasy. In the blink of an eye she crossed her legs and moved as far from me as the limo allowed.

"Mr. Marshall, you almost had me, she said as her hands fanned her face trying to regain composure. Damn, you're not shy at all once you get going."

"It's your fault, looking all inviting with your legs half open, your mouth open, perfume driving me insane. What's a drunk guy to do?"

"A drunk guy's going to wait. Trust me when the time comes you will be a happy whipped camper long before the pussy takes control. I have to be sure my man will be my man through thick and thin and not a fake. Besides, you have to know I don't always look this good, well most of the time I do but that's beside the point. Sweetheart, think of us as a roller coaster ride," she is inches from me, her soft seductive voice describing in detail of mounting anticipation, the rises and dips of a prolonged magical journey bringing us to the top, the ultimate high fed by love and desire. The drop is a never ending thrill that lasts for a lifetime.

The next day I got my car taken care of, only needed a new battery. Sometimes a kick in the butt or a new woman in your life will make you have more incentive to take care of business. Tuesday after work, I called Risha and informed her we were going to dinner. My question of where to come get her was answered with take a cab, we'll use the limo service. That woman's got the best perks I've ever seen. So started the most interesting month of my life. I don't know if both of us were in need of affection or if it was meant to be. All of the usual romantic cliché's worked magic on us.

Day One

THE SUN WAS warming up the day to a moderate seventy-five degrees. It would be a shame to waste a beautiful day in a restaurant, so I brought the restaurant to the park. When we got there, Risha was blindfolded and told to trust me. She pouted for a minute before doing as I asked. Once we arrived at a selected spot she removed it to an unexpected surprise. A look of bewilderment crossed her face until the realization hit at who the female was standing before her. She stood up and kissed me deeply then pushed me away.

"That's the last time I will ever kiss a woman, she cried out in laughter. I see you don't forget so easily." It turned out to be an excellent picnic.

Day Ten

"WAKE UP BRIAN." I hadn't spoken to Risha at length other than are you all right and I miss you since our picnic. It was three o'clock in the morning and I had to be at work by eight and then to practice.

"Are you all right," I answered trying to shake the sleep out of me.

"I am, but you're not. Call your job and take off, we're going fishing. Meet me at the bay in an hour and honey don't be late. I got ready to call her back but thought, why not, I never play hooky from work so one hour later I was pulling up to her friends boat.

"This is a fishing boat?" The Mistress of the Ocean stood 80 feet long and Forty feet tall overshadowing all the real fishing boats docked nearby. Twin 600hp outboard motors sat purring, anxious to show off the power they possessed. A tall man, muscular in stature, maybe six feet four, dark with beautiful smooth looking skin stood next to Risha. They looked too familiar standing there together as I walked up. His dress, silky blue and white uniform topped off with a white captains hat sitting on his baldhead conveyed a look of aristocracy. He greeted me by name with a more than firm handshake forcing me to exert more strength in my response. I said my hellos but could not for the life of me ignore the slight feeling of jealousy growing in my stomach. He put one hand on the aluminum ladder and helped Risha up with me following suit. I whispered to Risha while Maximillian nicknamed Maxi, prepared for departure.

"That is one good looking man." Risha giggled.

"You want to ask me if we are old bedmates don't you?"

"Well now that you mention it?"

"Do you think I'm classy, sweetheart?"

"Yes."

"Would a classy woman bring you around her old partner?"

"No."

"Of course not." There was no animosity behind her words, no feeling of being scolded, just a corrective conversation. And I felt a whole lot better having had such a conversation.

A small table for two sat on the front deck of the boat draped with a red satin tablecloth. The soft glow from a small candelabra made for the perfect romantic setting. Sitting next to it was a basket of mouth watering fresh cut fruit waiting for my appetite to make short work of it.

"After you, I bowed as I pulled out her chair."

"A gentleman, hope he's not around all morning?"

"I think he's already walking away, Ms. Allerton." The deep rumble of the engines signaled our journey had begun. Maxi cruised around the majority of boats actually going fishing until he could open up the outboards to twenty knots and head for the blackness of open water. Not wanting to waste a second of our time together we danced slow and sensual already lost in the music softly playing through the speakers built into the framework of the boat. The darkness of the night enveloped us as we left all the lights and excitement of all the other real fishing boats behind.

Her head rested in the nape of my neck as we swayed to the music under a starlit sky, watching white foamy waves leave a constant trail as it pursued the boat in almost mathematical perfection. A shooting star caught my attention prompting a superstitious belief to make a wish, one that while kept secret to myself I hoped to be fulfilled. We retreated to a plush bench at the rear of the boat, where away from our captain's eyes the real action began. She read my mind as we locked into each other in an attempt to break our marathon kissing record from a few nights back. I tried to cheat by sliding a hand down toward her breast. She let it get but so far before she bit my tongue and held it firm until I removed the foreign appendage. The romantic ride ended too soon with unfulfilled passions leaving us to look forward to the time when our urges will be satisfied in every way.

The blaring siren of the boat's horn warned of its approach to the dock never once disturbing a huddled pair sleeping peacefully in each other's arms as the yacht noiselessly aligned itself with the dock. A lingering kiss and a forgotten basket of fruit to eat in the car ended a near perfect romantic morning minus the sex. I spied a super stretch limo next to Risha's limo as I made my way down the ladder. A very pretty woman stepped out, long hair, expensive clothes, short skirt, and high heels like she was headed to a party. I thought it might be one of Risha's friends I saw that day on the train. Maxi hurried to greet her with the kiss and hug of a boyfriend. They walked over to us hand in hand when in true drama style, her hands go up to her face as she screams

Risha's name. They hug and kiss-kiss on both cheeks until Terri remembers I'm standing there and examines me with devious eyes licking her lips all the while.

"Maxi didn't tell me he had you and your new mm-mm-MM, beau out for a little moonlight cruise. If I could have been the fly in those drawers, I mean wall. Terri wiggled her fingers on a hand held out waiting for my attention. By the way handsome, I'm Terri. I took hold of her hand as she did a prolonged top to bottom inspection. There was nothing out of order with this chick. Her make up and hair was perfect, not a strand out of place. Long manicured fingernails patted her chest as she spoke. Don't take your eyes off this one or he'll get swept up. I'm going to dream about you tonight honey." I looked at Risha to be sure. An almost imperceptible nod was my answer. Yep, she was a he. Without missing a beat I raved to Maxi how much fun I had and that we must do it again real soon.

"You and of course Risha are welcome anytime," he answered.

"You two are on the permanent invite list," an over exuberant Terri added. I called Risha from my car.

"Thank you for a great start to my morning."

"I wanted you to go home with me on your mind and in your head."

"No thank you, that's why I'm going to work and where are you going as if I don't know."

"To work as well, will we ever learn?"

"God, I hope we do and soon. By the way, are we still on for tonight?"

"Yes, one good turn deserves another."

"Oh and you could have told me Maxi was gay."

"Maxi is Gay, Muah, bye."

Dinner was my choice and the movie hers. I wore a black tee, sweats and sneakers, super casual. Risha showed up in a mid drift, skirt and flats, always super sexy from any man's point of view. We feasted until food was no longer an issue but with an hour to kill before our movie a small surprise happened by way of a hidden park bench surrounded by bushes. Her legs swung back and forth as they hung off mine, their naked beauty enticing me to do more than enjoy her free spirit act. We basked in the anonymity of being unseen by people passing by us no more than a few yards. Risha, in a careless act of promiscuity and beating me to the punch flipped around and sat on my lap facing me.

"So you're going to drain all the restraint I have left."

"Remember this morning, she asked with lips a millimeter away from mine, this is the continuation." Her tongue slid through my lips maneuvering its way through my mouth to once again claim what was hers. This grind unlike that on the boat sent shockwaves through me. I wanted to fight, get her off of me because I knew nothing good would come of this, but in the end the quiet panting I did with each movement gave evidence of my enjoyment but not because I wanted to. People walked by within feet of our public display, oblivious to the sexual onslaught I was trying to avoid. My hands gripped her legs as an internal fight ensued to push her off and keep her on. We knew my willpower was gone so she too began making little panting noises as her pace quickened.

"Oh my god Risha stop. She ignored my pleas and rode my straining manhood while I struggled to keep it contained to the very end. Goddamn," I said knowing I'd been bested on our non-contact sport. She stopped when it was certain there was no more manhood to rock on.

"Goddamn, Is that what I heard. Did you make a mess in your pants young man?"

"HELL NO! Of course not," I lied. I was embarrassed for myself. Who knew I could get so aroused to the point of no return. She laughed, seeing a small wet spot appear on my sweats.

"Okay have it your way but do you at least want to go home and freshen up."

"That means we'll have to catch a later movie."

"Do you have a curfew?"

"All right, let's go and freshen up." When we got back to my car, she giggled.

"Did you think I would let you get away with wearing sweat pants and not try you out? Truth be told I need to freshen up myself."

Never thought about being ashamed of where I lived until we crossed that imaginary railroad track line. With the green signal of a traffic light we were at once in a very different environment. Risha was quiet like a child riding through a place never seen before. I glanced over to see her looking out the window wide eyed with curiosity. My car shook as I made my way through a maze of potholes marking my passage into South End. Things I never paid attention to were very much in my face now. We stopped at a light where some guys sat on crates playing a lively game of dominoes with a stack of money on top of a makeshift cardboard table. Halfway down the block was Angelo's liquor store where alcoholics hovered around it like they were giving away free drinks. We passed apartment buildings in different states of disrepair adorning the landscape within some blocks. There were many more liquor stores abutted to store front churches, abutted to barbershops, abutted to more bodegas, abutted to hair and nail salons, abutted to apartment buildings. The formula repeated itself in different variations from block to block. The streets too were filled with people doing what they did best, surviving.

"Ask away," I knew she had questions and why not, she was a long way from home.

"You think you're so smart, she laughed. You don't know where I grew up."

"Your whole demeanor said it all."

"Well, I am curious. We are in the ghetto now, right?"

"Yea, you could say that."

"It's a lot of us in the ghetto, hunh."

"Not used to seeing your own color everywhere?"

"I'm used to a mix of people but they are not all in the street at one time." I laughed.

"It's a hot day and those cramped apartments get very hot in the summer."

"Can't afford air?"

"Actually, most landlords don't allow it. Too much strain on the load coming into the building."

"Oh, I see, I see. Very interesting."

"What is?"

"Everything. I like the extreme differences in us." Her attention stayed glued to all the activity in the street, questions continuing to be asked and answered until I parked. We went the two flights up to my apartment where she made herself at home immediately.

"I expected left over take outs and dirty clothes everywhere."

"Why is that, I said a little surprised?"

"You a man."

"All of us men are not like the status quo. I happen to like coming home to a rat free apartment."

"What about roaches," Risha cried out as she put all her energy into squashing the intruding insect.

"Damn, didn't expect that. The exterminator was just here a few months ago. I guess I'll have to call up management again and have him do a repeat spraying."

"Don't sound so apologetic, this is a big building. I know there is a nasty single man in one of these apartments."

I got into the shower still shaking my head at the inability to control my little brain shriveled up between my legs. Don't hide now, I scolded. You need to control yourself more, you know I don't like being embarrassed.

"BRIAN," Risha shouted five minutes later. I ran out of the shower wet with nothing but a towel held together around my midsection. I had assumed she spotted a mouse this time.

"Is everything all right?" Risha put her hands up to her mouth.

"Look at you, boy if I had a thingy it would be hard right now."

"I hope you don't have a thingy, soft, hard or in-between or we gonna have a problem."

"Still have gay issues?"

"I never had gay issues, I just don't want my lady to be a man. I readjusted my towel and tried to look at ease. What did you want, woman?"

"Oh, just wanted to tell you next time I come here I expect to see a picture of us on this table." I looked at her for a moment before disappearing back into the bathroom.

Hard rain pelting against the window served as my alarm in the morning. Risha and I had planned a day of golf but an indoor activity of which I am prepared to suggest might have to suffice. Mother Nature got her accolades for the intervention since playing golf did not sit well with me. Getting beaten by a woman, no matter that I am a beginner and she wasn't is still wrong. Things were in place here so the only thing left was to pick up a few movies and we'll be set.

"You ready? Her sexy cell phone voice asked."

"I'm going to pick up videos as we speak, anything you want to see."

"You do know we're going for a walk."

"You do know it's raining cats and dogs?"

"Really, and here I thought it was snow."

"Funny, I thought black women and rain didn't mix."

"I think that's what you'd like to believe. OH MY GOD, is your other brain thinking for you right now?"

"NO, we just have a misunderstanding."

"You men always listen to the little brain and it always leads you into trouble."

"Am I in trouble."

"You're not, but that little one, he hasn't learned yet who has the power."

"Please be gentle is all I ask."

"We'll see when the time comes."

The country club was spread out over 500 acres of land and proved to be a perfect place for a romantic walk. I almost expected to see a lion or two as Risha held on tight while the rain bombarded our super wide umbrella to form a cascading waterfall around us. The rhythmic tap tapping of the raindrops set the tone for a leisurely walk through a private Garden wherein grew an enormous variety of flowers. Chipmunks, squirrels and birds went about their business as they would any other day, stopping for a second to shake off excess water then picking up where they left off. I poked my head outside the confines of the umbrella to enjoy the hot droplets of water massaging my face. Coaxing Risha to do the same, we soon had the umbrella closed allowing the torrential rain to soak us to the core. Risha enjoyed a moment to herself sitting on a rock, long hanging locks of hair funneling water in every direction, she seemed far away in thought removed from the present to reside if just for a second in peaceful solitude.

The following morning I got a message to expect a surprise. Between a banging headache and the sniffles, a surprise was the last thing I wanted. My job got the call out, medicines were set out on a tray and I was back under the covers. My plans of stopping this cold dead in its tracks was a foregone conclusion that worked out fine for killing the cold but by the end of the day it had escalated to the flu. Risha sensed something was wrong when she hadn't heard from me all day after the message she sent and before nightfall she was standing over me.

"Hi baby, I brought over some good ol' chicken soup for my man." Risha had let herself in with my spare key. I looked at her through mucus-veiled eyes.

"What you doing here, Cough, Cack," I canceled. I was in no mood for company but by now she wasn't company, still I was in no mood.

"Where does it hurt baby?"

"Where you think, I answered annoyed, ALL OVER." I was miserable and if Risha insisted on being here then she would have to be miserable with me. My response was ignored as she propped my head up on the pillow, felt me up and stuck a thermometer in my mouth.

"Just what I thought, you are burning up, she mumbled with concern in her voice. I brought some alcohol to cool you down after you drink your soup. Here, she put a spoon of cherry red liquid to my lips, take this medicine."

"Who comes down with the flu in the summer," I whined. Risha removed my tee shirt and got to work rubbing alcohol on my chest, massaging it in with a soothing circular motion.

"Do I still get my surprise," I said in a nasal tone saturated with phlegm. Risha, shaking her head put down the alcohol and raised her top to show off a thin satin black bra. Reaching for a quick feel got me a slap on the hand.

"This sweetie is all the surprise you're getting until you are better. A weak smile of appreciation crossed my lips as she lowered her top back down. Risha mothered me for three days while I carried on like a baby. On the fourth day I felt like a new man well enough to go to work. Risha had left the night before to take care of her own business but made sure I was okay before she exited. I tried to kiss her but she held up her fingers in the sign of the cross.

"Back man with flu, I rebuke you. Here take this," she laughed as she blew me a kiss on her way out the door. At work I couldn't stop thinking about this incredible woman.

>Thank you for everything Baby< was the text message I left on her cellphone.

>You're welcome honey< came the reply text five minutes later.

>I guess now you've seen me not at my best<

>Yea, you were a baby, still want you though, think you're well enough>

>Oh yea, I'm well enough< I texted her back as fast as my hands could type.

>LOL, you could be on your deathbed and you'd still claim you were well enough<

>If I weren't well, sex with you would certainly cure me<

>Sweetheart, if you weren't well, sex with me would definitely kill you. Anyway, I'll call you later< Later could not come fast enough.

Risha called me in the early evening.

"Brian, you home?"

"Where else would I be, I answered unable to mask the excitement in my voice. Where are you at?"

"I'm right outside your door," she said.

"What." I hurried to the door and flung it open. As I did, Risha grasped the long black knit sweater she was wearing, opened it wide and let it drop to the floor revealing a deep red pantie, bra lingerie ensemble that gave my imagination the boost it needed.

"My sweater baby," Risha reminded all the while sashaying her beautiful black behind toward my bedroom. Snatching her sweater up, I did a little dance into my room to my destiny. She was under the covers, the lingerie having served its purpose was flung across the room where they would lay for the better part of a week as my souvenirs.

"I'm waiting Brian, she hinted with the expectation of a queen waiting be pleasured, and please no foreplay, we've done enough of that to last a lifetime."

"Even better," I said while I assumed the position. I was more than ready or over eager as some would call it and therein lied the problem. Hard enough to jack hammer a sidewalk one second, the next, soft as an airless balloon. I was embarrassed, upset and still horny. My baby as all women do knowing full well I dreamed of this moment, that nothing and I mean nothing short of death would keep me away from consummating our night together, asked me what was the problem. There was no need to take my sudden temporary dilemma out on her so in the calmest voice possible, I explained.

"My manhood was erect off and on for most of the day, I began. Thinking about you and the anticipation of this moment takes a toll, if you know what I mean. No matter how hard I tried to take my mind off of tonight, I found myself still hard. Between being nervous and excited I think I may have overloaded myself and that grand entrance although an extreme turn on, one that I've never experienced before didn't help my control at all."

"It seems like I'm first on the menu then, so get on down there and have a meal on me."

"Anything you say, I said with renewed enthusiasm. Talk about the greatest woman in the world. Lay back and let me do all the work."

"Oh, don't you worry about that, I intend to."

Risha closed her eyes and fell silent in joyous anticipation. My intent was to approach this endeavor with the patience of a pro. I was not only trying to build her up to a point of begging for more, but I wanted to know every inch of her body. My tongue lashed out first starting at her lips. I pushed through to a receptive tongue waiting to engage mine. After a minute or two I pulled away and explored other areas such as tenderly kissing her eyelids, cheeks, and her ears. My hands touched all that was kissed, something of a blind man committing to memory all the beautiful features he feels. I descended lower reminding myself not to rush. Soft moans gave me an indication of her mounting desire and the need to take it up a notch. I purposely stayed on the fringes of my target taking advantage of my hold on her, while I sucked each and every toe at my leisure, then the massage of her legs fulfilling a promise I made to myself that I would finish what I started. Her magnificent breasts knew they were fondled when I finished with them, her erect nipples showing the telltale signs of excitement while I sucked them as I did her toes. She was quiet, save for balled up fists closed so tight veins made their appearance on her arms, showing she was right with me in the moment. A flurry of tongue sweeps on her pubic area prepared my target for a sudden shove of my tongue inside of her and licked with the purpose of hearing a scream somewhere along the way. Risha clawed at the sheets in a vain attempt to clutch something, anything to help get through her delicious torment. She locked her legs with my head in between to keep me stationary, forcing me to concentrate my efforts on one area. In a desperate attempt at getting the most out of my tongue invasion her body arched up until she emitted this low guttural moan mixed in with a release of her fluids. My head was held in its place until the tremors died and she was able to relax again.

"MY GOD, that's just what the doctor ordered, was it good for you too," She asked in a sarcastic tone?

"As a matter of fact, I enjoyed it as much as you, but I got your feeble attempt at witticism."

"Yea well, if you think you was good, wait until I'm finished with my turn, she said with a push. Lay back and close those eyes. What's good for the goose is good for the gander." What a silly idiom, I thought but damn if it don't sound sexy as hell at the moment. Risha got right to work kneading me everywhere except where it mattered most. Her touch felt good and I closed my eyes as per her instructions so I could get the most out of her massage. I opened my eyes in bewilderment when I felt lips clamp down on me. She looked up with a mouth full of me and commented,

"I couldn't wait." That worked for me. I wasted no time rolling Risha on her back to insert myself as far as a fully erect seven inches could go to experience the indescribable feeling of joining with someone for the first time. Although my wish was this moment would last forever, we raced to our goals of fulfillment together yet separate. I had a tight hold on her as I consistently pumped to a tempo my little brain choreographed. It was all I could do to hold on long enough for Risha's orgasmic ending which didn't take any time. We rode each other hard to the very last satisfying end to a reward of extreme relief. I held her tight, unable to withdraw until my convulsive trembling died down. Risha lay in my arms looking like, well, fucked. Her hair went in different directions, lipstick smeared and basic disarray but in a good way.

"You know, I'm thinking next time we make love."

"I agree, she said, but this, this was good, I need more repeat performances of this.

You know most men I meet, well, all men I've met until you, can't wait to tell me how much of a man they are in the hopes it will make them more attractive to me. I think If you feel like you can't get the job done without telling me up front what kind of macho man you are then you lack the self confidence to date me."

"Hmmm, I'll keep that in mind.

"Too late baby, I'm turned out."

"So now I can brag about my sexual greatness in the bed and my super intellect out of it?"

"Uh honey, don't brag, you still need some work on the sexual greatness part."

"Wow, Step on a brother's ego to keep him trying hard to please. Is that it?" She started laughing,

"If that's what it takes to keep you delivering performances like that last one then I'm gonna stomp that ego in the ground." We both laughed.

"Oh, and Risha?"

"Yes Brian?"

"Don't come here alone again, especially dressed like that."

"Dale brought me all the way to your door then left."

"Oh. Still no." Risha fell off to dreamland and I soon followed lulled by her calm breathing on my chest. Risha woke up first.

"Brian, are you sleep?" she whispered directly in my ear.

"Not anymore, is everything all right?"

"I was wondering?"

"What, you ready for round two. I could feel the stirrings of another erection coming on although sleep was still holding a tight grip on me. All my energy had not fully returned from my bout with the flu a few days ago. I drifted back to sleep in mid sentence. Risha pinched my nostrils together.

"What, what." I sat up.

"Get dressed, I want to walk."

"Woman, it's three in the morning."

"Sounds like a good time to enjoy the quiet of the night."

"Maybe you didn't hear me say before, it's dangerous out in those streets."

"I thought you said that because of the way I was dressed."

"Yea that and,"

"Come on, I want to see if the ghetto is like what I see in the movies."

"Sweetheart you're in the ghetto."

"I mean at night. Let's make a deal, we explore your neighborhood, then come back here and I give you what you want."

The moon was close to the end of its shift when we started walking. We held hands like teenagers without a care in the world except the good feeling of being in each other's presence.

"What's in that direction," she inquired breaking the comfortable quiet.

"Down that street and beyond is the beginning of the bad side of town."

"I thought you lived in the bad side."

"I do, but that is the south side which is worse."

"I don't see anything." I started laughing.

"Where are you from again?"

"Why, do I sound that dumb?"

"Not dumb, a little ignorant I guess."

"I know, I was sheltered most of my life. My mother made it her business to home school me so I'd be out of the streets. Where we lived wasn't the best of areas either and me being her only child and a girl, she was afraid."

"Your mother did a good job. Seems like you've done pretty good for yourself since then.

"Yea, I do okay. You never asked me what I did for a living, why not?"

"I asked you once but you side tracked me so I left it alone. I figured when you were ready to tell me you would.

-See over there. All that is gang territory," I pointed towards it as if we were standing at the gates of hell.

"Let's go down there and walk around. I want to see some gang members for myself."

"Risha, it's more to it than that. They're not animals in a cage although some of them need to be locked up. They live like ordinary people, it's just that with them violence can pop up at any time."

"So who's to say it'll pop up this time. Let's go."

"I don't think so. Why tempt fate. Most of the members show no respect for their life or anyone else's. Starting shit with people is fun to them and bad for their victims. You're really good looking and believe me when I tell you someone is going to say something or try something. I will wind up in a fight and the whole gang will show up in a matter of minutes to get at me and probably you too."

"Awww, you just scared," she joked.

"Damn right I'm scared and your butt should be too." I stood back, my baby was sexy as hell with her skintight jeans, Pearl necklace, diamond rings, big diamonds at that, platinum bracelets and diamond earrings. Others would see a walking money machine waiting for the right person to cash in. I would guess this is one of the down sides about being sheltered, you're clueless.

"Hold on, I said as we walked back to the front of my building. Stay right here, I'll be right back." I ran up the stairs like a jackrabbit found what I was searching for and ran back to her.

"What did you have to get?"

"A little help if needed," I answered patting my back pocket.

"You know what, I don't want to tempt fate." We began our late night walk anew and not towards the south side. I enhanced my gait to a cocky kind of stroll to show I was one not to be messed with.

"This is where the Batton boys had a shootout with the police, I indicated. Five people died right here on the sidewalk and that stoop." As we walked further down the street dried blood stained the sidewalk pointing the way to the bodega where the owner was killed two weeks ago as he opened up.

"Really, and you said that other area was much worse. I need you to move out of here."

"I'm sorry, all I'm telling you is the bad stuff." There were many good memories also like the different games we played, the many neighbors that believed in that saying it takes a village to raise a child, outdoor barbeques on the sidewalk. The warm summer's breeze and the walk down memory lane had a feel good effect on me and I enjoyed sharing it with Risha on my arm. After another fifteen or so minutes I announced the tour was over. We made a U turn in midstride and found ourselves looking at four young men. Damn, I thought, any other night there wouldn't be a soul out here.

"Hey pretty woman, you got five dollars." Risha answered before I could say no.

"Sure, give me a minute." While she dug in her purse three of them were focused on me while the fourth and smallest was in awe over Risha's breasts.

"See something you like," I asked in a tone dripping venom.

"It's all right honey. Here take ten." The nervousness in her voice was unmistakable but the money from her outstretched hand went untouched.

"Yea honey, it's all right, the short man mimicked. We conducting business HONEY so shut the fuck up and let your woman handle her transactions. Baby, that jewelry you're wearing looks expensive so give me that and all your money. The short man moved in closer to take Risha's necklace, but I stepped in front.

"Look, she'll give you the money and jewelry but you can't touch her." I held my hand behind me beckoning for Risha to put her jewelry in it. She stuffed it with her belongings but I knew it wasn't going to end here. Knuckleheads looking for trouble seldom are satisfied unless you know one of them or a friend or family member and sometimes that didn't make any difference either.

"I thought I was talking to your bitch. I tell you what, Shorty looked around me to Risha, if you walk your fine ass over to me, we might not beat the shit out of your ex-boyfriend."

"Fuck you, the only bitch out here is you."

"Motherfucker, you ain't a part of this conversation no more, fuck him up."

"STOP! Please, just take the jewelry and leave us alone."

"Too late for that, shorty said, me and you about to get better acquainted."

"Not in this lifetime.

Here baby, I put everything back in her hands, hold on to your jewelry and back up to the car." Risha was so paralyzed with fear I had to shove her gently in the direction I needed her to go. Scream if one of them gets near you. She shook her head but didn't utter a sound. The hairs on my neck stood up in anticipation of what was to take place. I stood with my fists closed in an awkward stance to give the impression, of someone who has never fought before. This was to make his boys think I would be an easy target. A onceover assured me there were no hidden guns protruding under shirts, and then Shorty got told some facts.

"No matter what happens here, you going to the hospital or the morgue, your choice."

"Yea, I don't think so." Two rushed at me to try and catch me off guard as their leader pulled out a piece from behind his back. It fast became a chaotic mess, nothing like in the movies where each choreographed scene lets the hero set up his defense and take on the foes in smooth fight sequences. Shorty was yelling for them to move out of the way while he waved the gun wildly about. My sticks were flying mainly on one of the men trying to hit me. His hands automatically went to his eye when after clipping him in the face, a nasty wound opened up above the eye. Shorty in all his wisdom couldn't wait for a clear shot so he did me a huge favor by shooting his partner in the back while we wrestled with a kitchen knife the man had pulled out of nowhere. I pushed the injured man toward Shorty and he pulled the trigger again missing both of us in his haste. Near enough now to disarm him, a hard pop to the wrist broke the delicate bone in three places forcing the gun out of his possession. I spun around at Risha's forty-decibel warning in time to receive a bat to my midsection, the suddenness of the pain forcing me down on one knee. Shorty was already running around parked cars trying to catch Risha who was using the cars as a barrier between them. I had to risk a second to gather myself but only a second thanks to Risha finding her voice again with another piercing scream catapulting me into action and not a moment too soon. Batman stood facing me, the tightly held bat in full swing on a collision course to the back of my head. Using my head as a battering ram, I sprang straight up, smashing into his chin with the force of a sledgehammer. I heard more than felt the crunch of teeth breaking inside his closed mouth as he lifted off the ground onto his ass, losing the bat in the interim. I punched on the fallen man until he was unconscious and still the punches wouldn't stop until Risha's non-stop shrieks sank into my crazed head bringing me back into sanity. Shorty had reached her but so did I to his surprise. He was thrown down from behind where I now started in on him. His eyes reflected the fear of me keeping my promise. He fought hard with his one good hand trying to escape my elbows to his face but to no avail. Blood splattered on my face from multiple gashes over his eye then under it. He moved his head around aggressively for relief from the pounding my elbow was doing to his face. Risha, not knowing what else to do was on automatic scream until my finger went to my lips. Shorty used this pause to roll under a car to the other side and run. I wasn't running after him knowing that straying too far from my terrified woman would not have been a good move. Wincing from my own pain, I picked up the abandoned gun and put it in my pocket.

"Come on, we need to get away from here."

"What about the police?"

"I'm sure they don't need us to figure out what happened and the rest of the gang might be here before the police so we need to not be here."

Minutes later we were around the corner, the serenity of it unbroken from the sounds of the battle that had taken place behind us. It was a struggle to keep up with a fast walking Risha who's head could not stop turning for fear of a gang member catching up to us. When we got back to my apartment, she made sure all three locks were taken care of then slammed down a beer from the fridge before collapsing on the couch. The couch pillow she substituted for a pacifier was forgotten with a quick switch into my arms when I sat down next to her. To tell the truth I needed the comfort as much as she did. With her face buried in the crease of my neck she bawled for ten minutes, jumped up, went back to the refrigerator, slammed down another beer, threw me one, then proceeded to the bathroom. I finished my beer and slouched down on the couch enjoying the fizzing sensation in my throat. Before Risha came out the bathroom I was sleep, awakened by the pulling on my tee shirt by Risha, intent on attending to my wounds. Her fears were confirmed with a gasp and a look of horror believing I was near death. The bat mark being the most significant of the bruises also hurt like hell. I said nothing but I was sure I might have a broken rib somewhere in there. She did what she could to wrap my body.

"We need to go to the hospital."

"Later, right now I want to rest." I pulled her down next to me, thoughts of what might have happened if things hadn't gone just right were bothering me. The evening's events were a bitter sweet pill, one being the proof of a real fight to show I am as good as I think I am and the luck of me fighting a bunch of idiots. The next chance I get I'm going to thank Mr. Hu and the guys for kicking my ass everyday at practice.

"I'm so sorry," She said.

"About what? Nothing tonight was your fault. We should be able to go anywhere at any time and that's all we did."

"Well, thank you from the bottom of my heart, Brian. You put your life on the line for me and, and, a new river broke out on Risha's face following a still damp route from twenty minutes ago.

-You Brian are a breath of fresh air. I said before you gave off good vibes and I was right. You're a HERO, my hero."

"Shhh, you're making me blush."

"You're too black to blush but you are everything I said and then some."

"Can't we talk about something else?"

"Right now, all I can talk about is you, my love."

"Well I know how to shut you up," I said as a shower of kisses caressed her face like so many flakes falling gently to earth.

"SEE, NOW I'm distracted."

"I apologize."

"Don't apologize honey, fix it," she said with a twinkle in moist eyes. We melted into one another, our need for each other's touch beyond our control. For Risha, this was a crucial release from a fright she had never in all her twenty-five years experienced. For me was the proof of being ready, willing and able to stand by her side no matter what, a man deserving of her love. There was no night, no day, no tomorrow, time stood still allowing our passions to spill over, consuming our very soul.

"Brian," she breathes my name, the sound pure and sensual to the ear, speaking volumes to what she craves. I hear her and I answer, my addiction for her running through me like a virus, filling every crevice with a love I had never known before. We are united together but the change within was evident. My love was pure and deep, she was my missing link. The experience, as horrific as it was, created a powerful bond between us that cemented us together. Salty tears were kissed away with a promise that I would never allow any harm to come to her. I had found my soul mate and losing her was not in my vocabulary.

"Now where were we?" Risha asked as she snuggled up close to me once again.

"I don't remember that but I do know this," I moved my lips inches away from hers.

"Oh no not again, Risha laughed as she put a finger in my mouth, suck on that for a while. So my super hero what else do I need to know or am I going to have to force you to show me like last night."

"I really don't think you want to find out anything that way again. I know I don't."

"No, I can honestly say this experience in one lifetime is more than enough for me."

"Yeah, Miss I want to see a real gang on their own turf. You were scared right out of your skin."

"Humph, like you weren't. I almost had to slap you into reality to get you to start saving my life."

"I think that piercing scream in my ear did the trick just fine. At least you know those diamonds you was wearing were real, cause if they weren't, pieces of glass would have been all over the ground." We both laughed until our sides ached.

Risha got up and looked on my bookshelf.

"X-men, Superman, Hulk. I see you're a serious comic collector. Is there some correlation between that and your martial arts training?"

"Well you could say that. I always wanted to make a difference in the world but until the other night I hadn't been a fight since school days."

"Damn boy, you coulda' fooled me. You handled three and a half men with no problem. I smiled, because she said it with so much seriousness. They were armed too, so that's double the men. Seriously, wasn't you scared?"

"I'd be lying if I said I wasn't. I thought there were no guns on any of them, which was a mistake. If you weren't there I probably would have run but..." Risha waved her hand to silence me and jumped back in the bed where we laid there entwined for hours making love when the mood hit. The nighttime sex was a repeat performance of the morning sex but time never stands still when you're enjoying something this much and in the blink of an eye it was over. Marriage crossed my mind and how I'm going to bring it up. I knew now was not the time so early in our relationship but for me, It will be soon. I studied her as she slept, wishing I could draw so my vision of her would be captured forever. I settled for a ton of pictures instead.

"What are you doing?" Risha's sleepy voice inquired, when she heard the camera click.

"I'm taking a picture of my future wife asleep. Smile." Risha gave a sleepy smile then turned over showing her bare ass.

"Take a picture of this," she indicated by moving her butt around. I snapped the picture.

"For the table?"

"You better not!" When we left the apartment twenty-four hours had elapsed after the incident. It was daytime and in no way did it look as foreboding as the other night. All the elements that make a person feel safe were around us. People were coming and going not paying us any mind, still Risha hurried up and got in the car.

...SIX MONTHS...

MY LIFE CHANGED gears in midstride as we got into the routine of sacrificing for the sake of love. I heard somewhere that being in love is hazardous to your health. I try to concentrate on my training, Risha is on my mind so what do I do, stop and call to hear her voice. I go to work, Risha is on my mind and not on the job at hand, which I've been warned about. When I go to sleep alone and wake up alone, Risha is on both of my brains. More often than not I have to relieve myself or I would never get any sleep. Her pillow remains untouched, her fragrance still intact for me to inhale as I slumber. When I know I'm going to see her I get butterflies in my stomach. I'm a different person when we're together. My imagination spans decades when we are old and gray with wrinkles everywhere. That thought is quickly squashed, black women don't age too much although I'd still live with her forever, regardless.

Risha called, saying she can't wait to see me tomorrow on account of her needing to be de-stressed. I told her I'm dying here without her.

"Please don't do that," she laughs. I said I love you just before she hangs up. I hear her say bye but that's all. Did she not hear me say it? Maybe her mind has changed in the last few months. Maybe she just has a strong like and a need for a sex partner only. I try to rationalize my thoughts, which seem to be running amuck. Is this a part of being in love, the self doubts. She doesn't say one little thing and I turn it into a major issue. I don't like this side of love. Thirty minutes pass since we spoke and I call her back.

"Hi sweetheart, she said, what's the matter?" I explain the situation and about her never responding back. She apologizes and reciprocates her feelings.

My thoughts turn to Mama and Pop. I hadn't been by the house since I met Risha. I talked to both of them on the phone sure, but Mama says she needs to see me. She says come by for just for a minute so she knows I'm all right. Mama didn't understand, to get up and travel to their house was over thirty minutes. I do wish I had gone over there at least once or mentioned Risha in conversation, because now there will be hell to pay. Pop would be no problem but Momma, I was her pride and joy since Russell. I decided to get it over with and drop in unannounced to spring Risha on her.

...MY PARENTS HOUSE...

"MAMA, ANYBODY HOME?"
"WHO'S THAT COMNG
IN MY HOUSE?"

"Who else has keys to this house besides me and Pop?"

"I do have more than one son." Okay, she's not going to make this easy.

"THERE you are. What's up pretty lady?" I can feel the chill as I kissed her on the cheek. Momma turned off the water and dried her hands before accommodating me.

"Let's see, I'm in the kitchen washing dishes dressed in unflattering house clothes. You show up out of the blue after I haven't seen you in months with the nerve to call me pretty, which as you can see is an outright lie, so what is it you need from me."

"I wanted to see you and Pop. By the way, where is Pop?"

"He's in the bedroom."

"Ok, I'll be right back and then we can sit and talk."

"I don't have any money," she called out after me.

"Don't need any." I sat down with Pop for a few minutes. I didn't need to beat around the bush with him and he would guide me on confronting Mama.

"I'm assuming you're in love with her and all that other stuff that goes with it so my answer to you is in pieces, son. Pop was sitting on the side of the bed clipping his toenails. He raised his head with a question in mind.

"You don't plan on getting married tomorrow, do you?"

"I haven't asked her yet. I'm buying a ring first."

"Tell her about the marriage another day. And for god's sake come by more often. Your mother gets on my last nerve worrying about you. Besides, I'd like to see you a little more myself. And congratulations, she must be special to rope you in."

Momma was seated with the TV tuned to some court show that she wasn't watching. Pop sat down in the cushiony armchair Mama bought him for his birthday ten years back. If Pop was home, that chair better remain empty no matter if he sits in it or not. That was Mama's rule and it was enforced to the letter. I picked up the second remote and switched the TV off.

"Did someone die," Momma snatched her spare remote and turned the TV back on. I glanced at Pop. He raised his hands. I sat across from her and started speaking above the TV. As soon as the word girlfriend was mentioned, off went the TV.

"She pregnant?"

"No."

"Is she the one keeping you from visiting." I looked at Pop again.

"Rose, that boy's got a life. He can't drop everything he's doing and come across town every five minutes."

"I'm not asking for every five minutes, ten will do."

"Mama I'll come by more often, I promise."

"So, when do we get to meet this girl?"

"She's out of town right now I lied but I'll let you know."

...JUNE 23...

RISHA PAID FOR the largest conference room at the famous Ivory towers at a cost of twenty five hundred dollars a night. It took up the entire top floor of the hotel and had its own private elevator. She took in the spacious room and shook her head in approval.

"This will do just fine," she noted as she visualized what changes were needed to meet her satisfaction. It was a challenging task but with her artistic background coupled with a team of set designers, the makeover should be complete in no time. Hours later the place had turned into a mass of organized confusion with props and workers everywhere. Risha barked orders left and right as she helped her vision become a reality.

June 24

12:01AM, HAPPY BIRTHDAY to you, happy birthday to you... First wishes, it was expected and to tell the truth, I was waiting for the ring. 12:02AM, call waiting showed Mama on the other line, the other woman in my life it would be to my advantage to never keep waiting. Risha understood up to the point of it being Mama but she was the only person besides Pop who had that kind of privilege, no one else. On Risha's suggestion I took the day off. She said the only real national holiday we all get every year is our birthday. I never looked at it like that before but it made sense so I took her up on the advice. She tells me after the fact we won't get together until later. My voice drops and she hears it.

"Don't worry honey, I won't miss your birthday. We're going to have a good time, you'll see." I'm still disappointed but I say okay. No plans on a Tuesday, which is a workday for any and everybody I care to be around.

"So what am I supposed to do while I'm waiting on you, sweetheart" and I say that with the hope of sounding pitiful enough to change her mind.

"Go and pamper yourself, that term isn't just for women." I think to myself, they need to come up with a different name for men then. That's been a feminine term for as long as I can remember, but I do as she suggests and visit the nail salon. To have a stranger holding the fate of each individual toe in their hands can be an agitating experience. The lady ignored my imagined anticipation of pain and true to the standards of a trained professional did a good job while talking me into a calm state. Maybe there was something to this being pampered thing.

Seven pm

"TAKE YOUR BLINDFOLD off sweetheart." The blindfold Dale made me promise to keep on in my elevator ride was one thing, spinning me around was another experience altogether. By the time the doors opened I was facing in the wrong direction barely able to stand straight. Risha cracked up at the sight, informing me that the spinning top thing was Dale's idea. The elevator stood fifty feet from the door where Risha stood wearing a red gown under a Golden Arch doorway with different colored lights flashing, 'HAPPY BIRTHDAY BRIAN.' Pausing to pick up a gift-wrapped box on the carpet, she blew me a kiss and disappeared through the door, leaving me alone with the box.

Remove all items of clothing, pants, UNDERWEAR, everything and put this on. I hope it fits, big man. When you are ready, you may enter at your own risk. Did I miss something, a loincloth and nothing else? What kind of celebration did she plan? Truly thankful for a private hallway, one can only wonder what the neighbors would have thought of my attire. I entered, taking my fate in my hands. As the door clicked shut, I found myself enveloped in darkness. At the sound of a clap the darkness was replaced by a black light highlighting an eerie almost scary looking landscape. From what I could see which wasn't much, it appeared I was standing in the middle of the jungle at night. Instead of furniture there was grass complete with trees, stars, giant rocks and if my ears weren't deceiving me a running brook. Sounds of different birds and animals could be heard now and again completing the whole scenario. I caught a glimpse of a large cat stalking me and almost had a seizure. It was my baby wearing a skintight black leotard cat suit designed to show every line and curve. She had a long white tipped tail, ears and whiskers. I figured I must be the prey so I hid behind a bush where I found a spear.

"Now who's the hunter," I said raising my spongy weapon high. The spear soared over her head, as her sudden leap caught me off guard, surprising me. We grappled for a moment until I was able to toss her off before she could sink those long claws into me and dove for cover. The lingering smell of perfume reminded me at how close she had gotten to making me her next meal. As dim as it was, those dangerous looking yellow eyes (thanks to contact lenses) shining like the beacon of death gave her away. For a moment I questioned my ability to defeat her in our impending life and death wrestling match. Then I heard it, a low rumbling growl signifying another attack. No more time for thoughts, action is required if I am to emerge the victor. I picked up a foam rock and smashed her in the side in a vain attempt at knocking her off balance. Injured, she still proved dangerous by taking a swipe at me. At one point we were nose to nose and I kissed her. She snarled her disapproval, spun around lightning quick and managed to extricate my loincloth while chomping down on my now exposed member. I froze for fear of losing an important piece of me. I knew now that I would not survive this, if I could not tame my ferocious feline. I began petting her in the ways only known to her kind. Before long I had my pussy purring with pleasure. Now fully aroused, she turned around and hiked her furry tail high, in anticipation of me finishing what I started. I acquiesced and mated with this beautiful creature thus cementing us together for life or maybe until time for the next meal. After hours spent in the jungle, dinner with friends sounded like the perfect idea.

My cat turned into a beautiful princess sporting a black and blue sexy mini dress with heels that put her eye level to me. Glossy blue lips and nails completed her look, matching her curly dark blue hairdo that was part of my attraction at our first meeting. She spun around once, stopped and waited for my approval. I motioned for her to spin again, this time to the left.

"Now spin to the right. Walk back and then forwards toward me." She picked up her purse, went out the door to the elevator and got on, never bothering to turn to see if I followed. I came up as the doors were closing.

"I thought so," she said with a slap on my head. We jumped in her waiting Limo and headed south to North Forks where dinner would be.

"What's this?" I asked picking up a small gold box on the seat.

"I don't know, why don't you open it and find out." I ripped open the box, acting like the excited child I was at the moment.

"It's a diamond ring."

"Yes it is and don't forget the garnet, amber, quartz, and emerald stones." She placed the ring on my finger and explained the meaning behind the four smaller colored stones as the four seasons in our lives. Winter, summer, spring and fall our love is what will always pull us through while the huge diamond represented radiating love which when bathed by direct sunlight reflected to the other stones causing them to glow. The inscription on the inside of the ring read 'Risha LOVES Brian'

"How am I doing so far," she asked like I must have had a birthday sometime in my past to compare this one to. As a matter of fact I would have never in my wildest dreams thought there would be another party to equal that one. It started off with a second hand car waiting for me out front begging me for a test drive. If that wasn't enough, on the table next to the car keys sat five thousand dollars, next to a chocolate cake, my favorite. The card read, your car to take you to the apt. you will be looking for and the money to get you started. Countdown to eviction is two weeks from today but right now, it's party time! By party time, Pop and Mama were a phone call away while I hosted the event of the year. The evening was made complete by the complimentary services from two girls in my class and still my birthday with Risha was by far the best. The night was still young and I was in a one upping mood that was going to make this birthday unforgettable.

We were soundproofed from the outside world, an appreciable aspect in setting the appropriate mood. The ring sat proud on my finger working the magic intended as it reflected small beams of colored light from the dome light overhead. I looked out the window past her, attempting to gather my thoughts and to mask what was on my mind until the last second. The scenery had changed to one of countless dashing trees blackened against a midnight blue sky through tinted windows. The time had come along with the lightheadedness stemming from overwhelming anxiety. With the keen sense of a woman who knows her man Risha's face turned to one of concern.

"Are you okay," she asked, feeling the instant change in vibes coming from me.

"Yea, I am but," I got down on my knee. Risha caught her breath as repeated whispers of 'Oh my God', flowed from her lips.

"I need to ask you something. Baby, you obviously have more than I could ever give you."

"What, hell no. Start again and this time you better be romantic. I smiled in spite of myself. It was supposed to come out better than that. I pulled myself together wishing for a really stiff drink, retook Risha's hands and tried to begin again.

"I assume I'm taking the long way?" Risha looked at me.

"Yes you are, thanks Dale." Dale made a quick right turn and turned on some music.

"I recommend something slow and mellow to memorialize the occasion. Hmm, Stylistics, you make me feel brand new, yes that should do it, old school, not over played. I had never heard of them before but they sounded better than what I had and it was a nice touch.

"That's fine Dale, you think you can roll up the partition?"

"It's jammed at the moment but don't mind me, you two keep doing what you doing, I don't hear anything." He started humming to the song as I restarted my proposal. Risha was tickled to death at my awkwardness.

"You two are not going to make this easy for me are you?"

"Am I not worthy, Mr. Marshall?"

"I'd have jumped out the window long ago if you weren't worthy. You are in fact very worthy."

"Well get to it already, we still have the second half of your birthday to get to." I took a deep breath.

"Risha, we've been together one year but in my heart it feels like a lifetime. I never in my wildest dreams thought I would find my soul mate. You make me feel brand new."

"HEY, that's good, you're adding the lyrics to your proposal, I like that." Risha rolled the partition up. Dale shook his head with a smile.

"Continue sweetheart." Risha's eyes were moist as she fought a losing battle to prevent mascara run. Her face told the story about a princess desperately waiting for those four small, yet powerful words from her prince to cement her place in his life and he in hers. I melted from the love I felt emanating from her heart and that gave me the words I needed to express what was inside me. My life as I knew it, is no longer valid without your angelic soul enriching it. My daily nourishment, my spinach, is you by my side. So I am asking you baby, I got down on both knees and Risha lost control. I carefully positioned her ring finger in my left hand, never revealing the ring in my right. We made eye contact and the words fell out. "Will you marry me, please?"

"Wait a minute, hand me a tissue honey. She wiped her eyes as best as she could then down rolled the partition. So Dale what do you think? Should I?" My ego took a huge dive at the referral of my question to Dale.

"Hell yea, I told you that weeks ago when you asked me what's taking him so long."

"There you have it Mr. Marshall, I'd love to. What'd you think I would say?"

"When you asked Dale, that hurt, no offense Dale. I didn't know this topic was discussed and decided without me. I wish someone would have been so kind as to inform me so I could've put all this nervousness and practice to rest. The ring was a perfect fit as it slid into its proper spot. She held it up at the light for inspection and then to Dale.

"Sorry honey but part of a man's duty is to sweat it out. It lets me know how bad you want that ball and chain locked around your neck. And by the way this lovely ring is worthy of my finger."

It had been six months since I mentioned Risha to Mama with no word about her since. I'd been by the house five or six times, stayed over once and our conversations were about everything but. I knew she would never appreciate any woman I was ever with which made me more skeptical about divulging our engagement. The last thing I wanted was a heated argument between us.

"Mama, I talked slow, needed time to think as I spoke. Remember I told you about Risha."

"Oh, the woman who is currently out of town."

"A dark night in hell! Why do you read all those science fiction books, you know it gives you nightmares."

"If I get a nightmare, I'll wake your father and you know him, I'm protected in or out of my dreams. Besides, we aren't discussing me now, are we?"

"No, well I have some good news to tell you."

"OH Lord, NOW SHE'S PREGNANT."

"No, not yet, maybe after we're married which will be in two months. -Say something."

"What do you want me to say? I'm happy for you? What kind of bitch dates a man for a year and never meets his Mama. I'll tell you who. A scheming, conniving, back stabbing, money snatching bitch, that's who."

"Mama, could you please not call her that."

"Sooner or later she's going to hook into your pocket and leave you wondering what happened. Trust me, I know."

"It wasn't her Mama, I didn't want any confrontations that would cause her to have doubts. She's always asked to meet you and Pop. Besides, she has more money than I could ever give her. "OH LORD, so you the gold digger."

"NO Mama, It ain't anything like that."

"Really? So you're saying, I'm the reason?"

"A little bit."

"Am I that terrifying, son?"

"You just stood here and called her every name in the book. What do you think, ma?"

"Brian you don't have to be afraid to bring your little female friends around. I'm sure I'll like them as long as they ain't like that last slut you brought up in here. Child was a crime against womanhood."

"She was fifteen and I was sixteen."

"They start younger than that these days, so am I going to meet this bride before the wedding?"

"Of course, next Saturday we're at her place for a first meeting dinner with parents and the wedding party."

"Oh good, and don't you worry, I'll know if she's the right choice after we meet."

"Mama, please don't embarrass me."

"Oh boy, hush up. Did you tell your father yet?"

"No, you tell him when he gets home."

"Are you going to tell your brother?"

"Yea, I'm going to see him tomorrow."

"I wouldn't advise you inviting him."

"How can I tell him and not invite him, besides, he's gonna be my best man."

"He'll be your worst nightmare."

"Mama, Russell is your son."

"Yes, and I know him better than you do."

"You never forgave him after he stole from you?"

"He stabbed your father and stole money, furniture, jewelry, you name it. Turned our whole life upside down."

"He nicked dad on the hand with a pen because dad was trying to hold him. You know he was sick and besides he paid for his crime, you're the one that put him away."

"Honey, ain't that much sickness in the world. You don't steal from family, PERIOD."

"Okay, let's drop it for now."

"Yea, don't say I didn't warn you."

Sometimes my mother can be so judgmental, like she never made a mistake before. The following day I found myself in a neighborhood I had no idea existed. My GPS seemed a little confused and only after reaching my destination did I know why. There were no street signs to get a bearing on exactly where I was so I kept doubting my trusty little instrument until I stepped out my car and checked a battered street sign laying on the ground in the middle of the block. Where there had once been a wall ending one street on one block and beginning another on an entirely different block, there was now debris. For once my GPS was right on the money. This place was known as hell's abyss. The inhabitant's, police, and anybody with any kind of criminal background knew about it or lived in it. Once Truman Street was located, the question of where to park my car was next. There were plenty of parking spaces on the block sitting vacant in front of condemned buildings that outnumbered the livable ones by two to one. Everybody in the street watched the car roll down the block making plans during my absence after parking. I wisely decided to park a few blocks away in a working neighborhood.

"You got a dollar," a young high-pitched voice of a boy begged more than asked. Under normal circumstances, the action of giving a kid a dollar would be second nature but with so many people waiting to see me reach in my pocket, no seemed to be the best answer for this situation. Fighting my way back to the car was not an appealing thought. I turned towards a group of individuals who watched me as though I was an alien.

"Excuse me, I'm looking for a man named Russell, anybody know him?" One old man jumped up scratching himself and repeated the name.

"Russell? You don't smell like a cop boy, what you want with him."

"That's my brother."

"Oh, now that you mention it, you look just like him, the old man smiled showing teeth that had seen better days. He pointed to a dilapidated apartment building across the street four doors down, and then held his hand out for change. I declined once again and walked the few yards to the building where a condemned sign tacked to the front was displayed. I hesitated a moment wondering if the old man along with his friends set me up. Standing at a door with no doorbell, secured with a broken lock on a corroded chain and with all eyes on my back, I attempted a light knock causing the door to fall down off the one hinge that failed to keep it up.

"RUSSELL, SOME MAN STANDING AT THE DOOR," a woman hollered without getting up. Russell appeared in a flash.

"Well, I'll be GODDAMNED," Russell spat out as he quickly replaced the stolen .38 he had pointed at me. What the fuck brings you here to the other side of hell." I almost didn't recognize him. It had been about five years since the incident and street life had taken its toll on his appearance. He lost a lot of weight from the big muscular man he once was.

…MY BROTHER RUSSELL…

NEVER TRUST A Dope Fiend, Mama lamented after the incident. He didn't start out like that. Nobody does. Russell is a victim of circumstance. In the world of high school sports, he was what they called a natural. That is a person who is born with a god given gift of being able to excel at any sport without trying. At fifteen he was placed in one of the top sports high schools in the State. His academic record read otherwise but that was not what he was there for. He was placed on the baseball and basketball Varsity teams because they were in desperate need of a savior to bring them out of a five-year slump. To the delight of the coach, Russell proved himself to be the myth come true. Records dropped like so many leaves from a tree on a windy fall day. Did I say he played on two teams in high school? He carried both teams all the way to be first place champions on statewide, countrywide and nationwide levels for two years in a row. Unprecedented right! Now add three gold medals in track and field and a B average in classes he seldom attended taken care of by female tutors who chose to do more fun things with him than tutor. The walls in the offices and in the hallways were once covered with mementos of his achievements. When media got wind of the phenomenal kid from West Eagle High along with scouts from around the country, the school's over priced tickets sold out in record time, most going to scalpers who demanded an even higher ransom. His autographed pictures also became a profitable commodity being sold exclusively by the school. From his coach to the principle, every win was an extra payday and I can't begin to tell you the gambling aspects of his arrival. And best of all from a young mans point of view, he had his pick of female students who were in contention with the female teachers for his attention. I guess a superstar at any level is a great find. Mama was so proud of him she allowed him to do whatever he pleased. If she had use of a crystal ball back then, Lord knows things would not have turned out the way they did. Right now, if you walked into that school you would never know he attended.

Towards the end of eleventh grade, things fell apart. You can't say no one saw it coming. Everyone tried to steer Russell in some direction conducive to his or her needs. Russell had teachers on one arm, his peers on the left leg, the principal and coaches on another arm and sharks, gamblers and dealers on his right leg. They all had plenty to lose, so it was in their best interests that Russell make it for at least one more year. Russell had his own visions of the future, which included in him making it to the end also. Scouts and the like had been filling his head with a pie in sky life for him and his family, but too much free time with no direction, in addition to the, can do no wrong power appointed him was Russell's downfall. While his peers were in school where he didn't necessarily have to be, he took to the streets to find something more to his liking. His choices, though fun for the minute were not going to be good for him in the long run. Street life sucked him in a little everyday, so minute it was unnoticeable. The major players in the criminal world needed to control him for their own illegal financial rewards. First he was given money for no reason other than being admired, to do with however he saw fit. His hangout spots, which were fronts, owned by drug dealers donated drugs for whatever mood he needed to achieve. Russell understood the fact that nobody else received money or drugs for free but he was the star and therefore privileged.

Mama and Pop weren't oblivious, they heard and saw things. My parents were true believers that being in the streets could either be a good or bad learning experience for you. It was all up to what you were looking for. School was never a major concern in the Marshall household. Mama and Pop did very well for themselves with neither achieving a diploma during their youth. This is why they didn't interfere with Russell's decision about seeking out other avenues. They both thought that since they were street life survivors, Russell would have inherited the good common sense that is vital if you were to come out on the upside when you were through running the streets. Neither they nor Russell knew he was already hooked on drugs. When a major shipment was seized, the abundance of drugs ended for a short time. Normally Russell wouldn't think twice about it until his body reminded him over and over that it now needed drugs, as it's main nutrient. Russell also gambled his way into a sizeable debt that he didn't want his parents to know about. The last thing he wanted to do was disappoint them. But like I said, it all went sour. Russell had traveled down a path, which could have but one outcome. After the major players were sure he was hooked, the slide downward was not only quick but deep. All freebies came to a swift end and debts were called in to be paid including the triple interest rates that accompanied these types of loans. Russell still thought he had a handle on things and refused to let his parents in on his problems. He agreed to a few deals that would put him back at square one free and clear. It started with point shaving and transgressed to throwing a few games. No harm done, everyone still wins in the end. Russell also stood to fill his own pockets with the promise of you take care of us and we will take care of you. He might have been able to pull it off if as we know Russell didn't have a habit. Because his abilities were so much more above average than the other players even when he played high, he was still the star they needed him to be. The topic of Russell's extra curricular activities eventually came up at a school board meeting prompting an impromptu question and answer session with one question key, on a long list of the admittance of everything he was doing except his addiction.

"Can you deliver another championship this year?" The answer by Russell himself,

"Hell yea. I want it just as much as you do."

"Okay we've heard enough. You're dismissed and we'll see you tonight and bring your 'A' game." They, being the coaches, the principle, vice principle and two high ranking members of the school board decided to play the role of the three monkeys for now. Dealing with Russell as compared to the massive amount of money he brought to the school was a no brainer. On the other hand, the decision to dump him after the season was finished was overwhelming. The writing was on the wall, Russell had to go before he ruined the integrity of the school's sport program. Russell one up'd them entirely by accident by going straight from the meeting to the drug dealer. Mama was at the game along with hundreds of fans waiting for number twenty-two. The game started with chants of, we want Russell and finished without him, to a twenty-seven, forty-three loss. The coach was more angry than worried, but Mama went to look for him alone. Russell was in jail for a number of charges his worst being the assault with a deadly weapon charge against a peace officer. This charge alone constituted denial of bail. He was there for a month before being let out. That year there were no championships and no school for him to return to. Mama and Pop being who they were took it all in stride as life's lessons. They put all their efforts in helping Russell get back on his feet until Russell gave up on Russell. He was insistent on doing what he wanted to do which was get high and hang out. Mama changed after that. She said life was too easy for Russell, made him lazy. All he wanted to do was play and let everyone else do the work for him. Mama stopped drinking and started paying closer attention to me.

I had envied Russell right up to the moment I laid eyes on him for the first time in years. I thought of my brother as a rebel who wanted to live his life the way he saw fit. The truth is a hard pill to swallow even when it's staring you in the face. I don't think Russell had a clue as to what he passed up or maybe he didn't care.

"Can I come in?" I asked.

"You already in Lil' Bro. You know you always welcome in my house." Russell's strength was still apparent in his hug as he put his arm around me and ushered me to the dining room where his friends were congregating.

"So what's on your mind little brother, Ma ain't dead yet, is she?"

"Nah, everybody's fine. I'm getting married."

"WHAT! Get the fuck outta here." Russell stood back a bit and looked me up and down the way old people did when they haven't seen you since you were a kid.

"Congratulations lil' bro," a female's voice sang out.

"Yea, congratulations," The whole table echoed as they continued with their business.

"Thank you." I counted six men and women sitting at the circular table mixing cocaine and heroin right out in the open as if it was a legitimate business they were working. The woman who yelled for my brother was the only one to look up from the task they were involved in. I forced myself to look away and to my brother who was watching me with a grin on his face.

"Gotta make that paper some kind of way. Ain't like the old days."

"Anyway, I continued, ignoring the statement like I would forget what I saw. I wanted to ask you if you would be my best man?"

"You motherfuckers hear that, baby bro wants me as the best man. Russell gave me another big hug. I would love to but I'm not especially prepared for the occasion."

"Don't worry we got time to get you straight."

"Sure enough, just tell me what I got to do and when."

"You got to be at a meet and greet dinner Saturday. I'll pick you up. Uhh, you have a phone?"

"Sure I do, we ain't that far back in the Stone Age. Russell snapped his fingers and Patricia, a bony girl of about twenty pulled out a cell phone and punched in the numbers as I rattled them off. She then rang my phone so I would have it in my memory. That number's good for about two weeks but I'll let you know when it's changed.

Risha and her mother were having their mother daughter talk about love and marriage about the same time.

"So momma tell me what do you think about Brian from what I've told you so far."

"Well dear, he sounds like a good catch but a woman of your caliber really should not be mingling with the lower classes. You need a man that is more like you."

"You mean rich and conceited."

"Yes, this man will be so busy loving your money, he won't have enough left in his heart to love you."

"He already loves me momma."

"NOW maybe, because he thinks you're poor like he is."

"He's not poor Momma, he's just part of the working class that gets paid less than I do for his work. You know Momma it hasn't been that long ago that we were like him."

"Yes dear that may be true but I produced a child that would pull her family up to the next level. That alone puts you and me in another category, which is wealtheee!" Less than satisfied with their talk, Risha let it stand as it was so she could enjoy her day.

Being the typical woman, she was at her best when it came to her first loves, planning and shopping. She became giddy at the mere thought she was in love with a man who not only wasn't from the same social ladder as she but was madly in love with her as well. He fell in love with her, not her name or the new character she portrayed in that silly show 'Another Day at Creston Lake.' She contemplated over the thought of him not having a clue as to what her job description was. Thanks to good luck she landed her part on the soap at the right time or it would have been impossible not to be recognized sooner or later. The bit part she started with was gaining popularity in leaps and bounds making it more difficult everyday to get around without being noticed. The producers acknowledged a ratings spike in the shows favor when Monique' appeared so the decision was made to change her bit part into a full-fledged character that was there as long as the interest stayed high. There would be no problem in that for as we all know sex sells, make believe or not. Add lies, cheating, and all the other little scandalous acts that raises an eyebrow and you have Monique'. Risha was praised constantly on the discovery of her great acting ability besides her job as associate producer. Since making her transition time passed quickly with nights dedicated to Brian along with days split between work and Brian. Who said you can't have your cake and eat it too? An irate woman threw a cup of soda at Risha, missed and hit a woman walking parallel to her. She had no time to explain herself to the woman who lashed out immediately. Risha kept walking choosing to not be a part of an ignorant person's retaliation. She could never get used to the viewers who lived their lives through a show. Yea, the time was ripe for spilling her secret to her husband to be.

The day before the dinner Russell had a date with me to help him look as though he rejoined the human race. He was on the corner looking his usual disheveled self but in this neighborhood, not out of place.

"RUSSELL, I called out as I pulled up to the curb. Was you out here long," I asked, searching for a way to start some dialogue going between us.

"Nah, nah, he replied as he searched up and down the streets as we made our way slowly through the narrow blocks. Hey, do me a favor and stop over there for a minute, he indicated as he directed me towards a shabby looking storefront. You got ten dollars," he asked with his hand already on the door handle.

"For what," I asked in a stern type of tone signifying my awareness of a drug front when I see one.

"Pack of cigarettes, he said unswayed. You know how these habits can be." Reluctantly I handed him a twenty and before I could say bring back my change, he snatched it and was gone. Damn, he sure moves fast when he needs to. Fifteen minutes later I got out of the car to look for him just as he shows up.

"What the hell kept you? I didn't need a brick upside my head. My money had gone to supply his habit. Now how the hell are we supposed to get anything done today?"

"Don't worry lil' bro, I'm sharp as ever."

"Russell, if you can take more than two steps I would be surprised."

"Just get me into the car, I'll be fine in a few." I locked him in his seatbelt as he went into a nod. So begins your day Brian, I say to myself. I step a little too hard on the gas, I guess on purpose. Russell straightens up,

"My man." He bends back into another nod. His hand goes to his face, I'm thinking to scratch an itch but it doesn't come down for a long time. I shake my head because since reuniting with Russell, I'm learning more than I ever wanted to know about drugs and the life lived addicted to them. I'm in take care of business mode now, got to concentrate on getting done and taking Russell back to his place.

"PARK THE DAMN CAR, IDIOT." I was in need of releasing some anger and this fool was the perfect candidate. His double-parked car was causing a major tie up within that one narrow block while he chatted it up with a woman at everyone's expense. The guy gave me the finger as I worked my car pass him and that's all it took for me to stop the car. Russell was in such a deep nod at the moment he wouldn't have notice if we crashed and burned. Calm down Brian, it's not that serious. The guy stood there shouting profanities like he was ready for a fight. Lord, we both know nothing good will come of it if I face him off out of this car, but the shouting match continued.

"Today's your lucky day fool, I got more important business to handle." He shouted something back, I'm guessing in the range of, "Fuck you."

"Idiot." Always some damn woman behind every foolish man who's trying to show his macho-ness for her attention.

When we arrived at the barbershop, I shook Russell awake.

"Let's go," I said, still angry that he got high on my watch and with my cash no less.

"What? Damn we got here quick lil' bro. Shiiit, that was a damn good nap."

"Don't you mean nod."

"Yea, whateva." The barber's chair had a royal feel to it, reminiscent of the good old days when Russell was the king of his peers. He leaned back into the head brace, his mind already drifting to some far off time when life wasn't so screwed up. The barber treated Russell like a piece of canvas that needed his expert attention to transform it or rather him into a masterpiece. It was the miracle I had hoped for but the final phase was yet to come. When we found ourselves at the door to the nail salon Russell exploded.

"Hell no, that's for gay niggers." I told him I used to feel like that too until my first time.

"Well count me out."

"Look at your fingernails. You can't go to a dinner like that. I bet your toes are in even worse shape."

"All right, all right, shut the fuck up." There's something to be said about being too high to care.

The nail salon was like any other with its distinct ambiance of Korean culture to give the workers some semblance of a home away from home. The location is what made the difference in clientele, which kept the place crowded from opening until closing. A young pretty Korean woman called for us to come sit in two recently vacated chairs. Russell took off shoes that had a piece of cardboard covering what used to be a sole and filthy socks with so many holes they were useless. The poor girls nose crinkled up from the smell so she hurried up and placed Russell's feet in soapy water.

"They got some pretty foreign bitches in here. What's your name girl," he picked up his right foot and pointed this big wet crusty toe in the young girls direction while she was preparing to wash his feet. The manager got ready to say something to Russell but was stopped by a customer. The girl mumbled her name but Russell's attention had already shifted to the huge mirror facing him that traveled the length 1of the wall.

"GODDAMN, I'm a pretty motherfucker. All heads turned. Shit Bro', Russell nudges me, I hope next on that to do list is get Russell some pussy. You know I can't let all this beautifying shit go to waste. The manager looked at Russell, disgust in her expression. Bad enough her girl had to tend to the filthy looking claws he called nails but now she had to endure his obscene behavior. Russell kept talking until she couldn't hold it in any longer.

"Sir, have respect for the women in this place, don't use that language in here."

"BITCH, MIND YOUR FUCKING BUSINESS AND DO YOUR JOB. AIN'T NOBODY TALKING TO YOUR CHINK ASS." I tried to smooth it over before the police were notified along with my apologies, but Russell kept yelling so we left leaving me to pay the tab for nothing much getting done. By the end of the day though we managed to complete my do to list with all the clothes minus the shoes staying in my trunk until needed. TV and a beer equal relaxation time but worries are seeping in just before I fall asleep.

...MEET AND GREET...

SATURDAY MORNING STARTS with a needed cup of fresh home brewed coffee. Three cups come and go without notice all due to my worrying about Russell embarrassing the whole family because I chose to include him. My decision to pick him up early to have a talk puts my mind at ease for the moment. If this is the prelude to a successful ceremony then I can understand why once in a lifetime is all that's expected. For now other things take priority, like the bathroom is calling my name or my stomach is calling for the bathroom. In any case I'm in there hoping for some relief. I don't rush it, there are so many things on my mind that this visit doubles for reflection time but it doesn't last long. Stomach pain interrupts my thought process, followed by cramps wreaking havoc on my inside. I hug my knotted stomach as I rock back and forth, my breathing stops for long lengths of time as I force a buildup of pressure. Welcome relief comes in a mixed tidal wave of excrement and urine surging into the bowl with the suddenness of a shaken soda pop. It wasn't nerves at all.

Two and a half hours before the dinner I arrived at Russell's to find myself wasting precious time waiting for him to come out of his dead man state. The usual group was there, ignoring my presence as they went about developing their product for the street. Every one looked like a dope fiend in one form or another and I wondered how much product actually made it to the public. I wander to the back to find Russell and get this show on the road.

"RUSSELL," I say his name loud hoping he stirs. It's a disgusting sight, this being my first time in the back area of the apartment. There are five others sharing this space all asleep, all in various stages of undress, all needing hot soapy baths to wash away some of the unbearable stench in the air. Garbage strewn in every available area blended its rotting aroma to human stink making for a toxic like poison that sent my gag reflex into convulsions. A laugh manages to sneak out when I count three garbage cans filled to overflowing. As anyone knows filth breeds a variety of insects which all are unpleasant. The room was alive with movement as roach armies fought for the right to spread more germs than their flying colleagues. Definitely never sitting on anything again if and that is a very big if, I ever stepped foot inside their doorway again.

My mind drifted for a moment to a show that used to come on TV called Scared Straight. It was about convicts showing up and coming wanna be thugs where they were headed if they kept on the path they were on. I don't know about them but this scene sure worked for me. If there ever was a life lesson that could scare a future drug addict straight, it would be to let them peek inside a day in the life of a true drug addict. A needle hung out of the arm of one woman like it was a part of her and Russell had a needle still inside of him also close to his groin. All were so malnourished I didn't see how they could make it another day. The mattress they shared, what part of it I could see, looked like it was taken off the back of a sanitation truck then dragged through the streets until it reached it's destination.

It was easy to get the wrong impression. The living room and kitchen areas had the bare minimum, a few chairs and a table. There were three crates stacked in the corner, I assume for company but that was about it. No one lying around, no garbage, only the baggers traveling back and forth to the bathroom. The real life shit like all bad things took place out of sight.

"RUSSELL wake up, we got to get ready." Russell stirred giving me that famous laugh he used to do when we were young.

"Ha, ha, yes, yes, yes, Let's go."

"First go take a shower, I said, and please take that needle out your leg."

"Yea put that somewhere safe," he hands me the needle. I take it with two fingers like it's carrying the bubonic plague or something. A thought crosses my mind,

"Russell is there running water here."

"We had it a few days ago." Shit, please, please have running water. I look around for the bathroom. In the kitchen where his workers are, one is psychic pointing me in the right direction. Bad news, the bathroom is much worse than the bedroom. The smell almost prevented me from entering but I take a few steps back, take a deep breath and enter. Green flies better known as shit flies spread out at my entry in preparation to defend their food supply that is to my utter revulsion when I see what they are protecting so vehemently. Shit is on towels, newspapers, the hands of the unconscious man in the tub, in and on the toilet is shit mixed in with garbage in brown standing water because the toilet is unable to flush. Knowing there is no water does not stop me from turning the faucets. Looking back at the tub, I whisper scream to myself.

"Anyone using the can," Russell appears in the doorway.

"Put some clothes on, we got to go." He says in a minute while I push past him eager now to leave. Damn Russell, you're not in the gutter, this is sewer territory.

Two hours had elapsed before we're ready but now he is raiding my refrigerator. The last beer is upended and guzzled down while his hands are touching everything in his search for lord knows what.

All that rushing and agonizing and we're the first ones there. I pulled the car to the end of the circular driveway and got out. It was a breathtaking moment to stand in front of my future living quarters in such a posh area. The brick house was modest in its appearance typical of the houses in this part of town. It sported the usual amenities well to do people enjoy, the best schools nearby, fitness centers, swimming pool, golf club, kayaking you know all the nice things nine to fivers get to enjoy once in a while at a cost.

"GODDAMN, you hit the motherfucking jackpot." Russell said, unable to contain his enthusiasm. I didn't bother to respond though I agreed with him and to tell the truth the wealth was still the most insignificant part of the jackpot. The sudden apprehension on Russell's face told me Pop and Mama must have rolled up behind me. When they exited the car Russell went over to Pop with his arms out apologizing about something that he thought separated them for years. Pop told him he had nothing to apologize for. Love for his family is unconditional and when he was ready to be helped his family would be there every step of the way including Mama. They hugged putting it to rest then Pop turned him to face Mama. Their exchange started off friendly enough with him being first to address her. Her reply,

"You ready?" Russell couldn't look her in the eye as he answered,

"I'm okay," the same reply he gave her years back when she first posed the question. He couldn't look her in the face then and now was no different. When it came to matters of Russell, Pop was the spokesperson due to Mama's impatience because Russell refused to try and get better. It was something she couldn't tolerate but knew all too well having grown up with an addicted mother. This issue kept them at arms length even though it was clear the love was there. Mama kept tabs on him through Pop and always made sure he had a working cell phone so he could reach out at a moments notice.

"Brian, you neglected to tell me your friend,"

"Fiancé,"

"Yes dear, your fiancé is rich. Are you sure we are at the right address?"

"Yea, This is the right address."

"What line of work is she in? I couldn't answer that because I didn't know nor did I care.

"Let me ask you an easy question. What did you say your fiancés' name was?"

"It's Risha, Mama." That was an easy question.

"Risha, Risha, mama hummed as she tapped her fingers against her face. Does this Risha have a last name son?"

"Allerton, you would not have heard of her, she isn't anyone famous."

"Son you wouldn't know famous if it slapped you in the face and fortunately for you it has. Risha Allerton is Monique from Another Day in Creston Lake."

"Trust me Mama, I know my Risha and a star she is not."

"Don't argue with me, I know I'm right. She's not a well known star yet because she hasn't been on the show long enough to have much of a following. The only reason why I know of her is because I watch that soap. Look Brian, this is a big expensive house in an area of famous people. If that isn't enough, her name is Risha Allerton, the same name on the credits at the end of the show," Mama finished off in that I know I'm right sarcastic tone. Five minutes goes by and Risha's gray Limo pulls up behind Pop's car in the driveway. The dark tinted windows prevented anybody from seeing inside but that didn't stop all onlookers who had gathered from staring in anticipation of the guest of honor. Dale stepped out and gave a nod.

"Friends with the driver Brian, and you didn't wonder." When he opened the door, out stepped two of the bridesmaids I remembered from the train. They were my second and third fantasies behind Risha.

"I see you read the note," one of them quipped. Seems she remembered me as well.

As Risha exited the car, she commented on what a handsome looking couple Mama and Pop were. I thought if Russell and me could come close to looking as good in our later years, we'd be blessed.

"Risha, it's good to meet you too honey, I don't know why Brian would keep a gem like yourself away from his parents unless he's ashamed of us.

"MAMA."

"Just kidding honey, Mama likes to joke a little from time to time. Between Risha and Mama throwing compliments at each other the mountain of crap was getting high enough to need boots. I looked at Pop with a smirk.

Risha talked a few minutes more then directed my parents to the house and pulled me back into the limo. She knew I was a little puzzled as she expected. She put her fingers to my lips and spoke.

"Brian my love, I've searched a long time for a man like you to complete a woman like me. When I first knew I liked you, I concluded that all I wanted you to see is a woman with a good job, simple as that. It's time you knew what I do for a living. I'm an associate producer for a soap opera and recently became an actress. Why you and not someone who is on my level of wealth and fame? I wanted a down to earth man who is okay with who he is. With you, I know I matter more than anything in this world. Most men from my social ladder wouldn't know anything about putting me first, last or through and through. Still the only way for me to be sure of us was to perpetrate this unfortunate ruse. I do not apologize for my actions because it led me to you and my falling in love. My answer once again is yes to marriage and I will try to make you a happy man. I will never deceive you again so all I ask is, please don't be angry."

"I always figured you were well off, it's who employed you that was the secret. I thought you were doing something that you were ashamed of although lucrative in nature.

"So who is this Monique, my mother seems so excited about."

"Well, that's my stage name on, Another Day in Creston Lake, ever heard of it?"

"No, can't say I have."

"Typical man, don't like soaps right?"

"Hell no. Anyway, between work and practice, I'm too tired to be bothered with TV."

"Don't forget about me in that equation."

"Hell no, you're before work and after practice then bed."

"I better start my own exercise program if I'm going to keep up with you."

"You better."

"Well anyway, Monique is a teasing spiteful home wrecker. She came on the scene six months ago and is making a mess of whoevers life she comes in contact."

"Believe it or not I'm still not interested at least not right now. Let's go get this party started." Risha smiled, she wasn't ready to drop the conversation just yet.

"Brian, It's not going to be easy being married to someone in my line of work. Everybody wants a piece of your time or a piece of your life, of which neither belongs to you anymore. Think about what you're getting yourself into and if your decision is not to get married, I'll understand."

"That's good to hear." Risha's face dropped. She turned away from me as she reiterated, her voice so small I had to strain my ears to hear.

"I understand."

"No you don't understand. You take my heart first and then you ask me to think about marrying you. Did you expect me to get cold feet? I meant what I said when I proposed so are we done now, cause I'm hungry."

"Thank you for forgiving me."

"Risha, It's not like you held back something bad. I'm marrying a movie star, how can I be upset."

"I've been a soap actress for six months now. Trust me, I'm no star. If you ask me, I think I made out better. I caught me a great man."

Russell leaned down and peered into the dark tinted windows, anxiety written across his face. I rolled the window down.

"I thought you had gone inside."

"I don't know anybody back there."

"Mom and Pop, oh never mind I'll be out in a minute." It's been a long time since he was around people unlike his friends so it made sense that he would feel out of place. Watching from a TV screen was all well and good but up front and personal is a lot to take in. Risha grabbed both our hands and stepped towards the crowd. We went in through the front door of her home where we were besieged by her friends and family members.

"Shit, she whispered. Brian, Momma…

"Oh, where is she?" I was anxious to meet my future mother in law.

"Momma doesn't approve of our getting married so I'm asking you to pay no attention to the hurtful things I know she's going to say."

"Don't worry woman, if I could win you over your mom don't stand a chance."

"Brian sweetheart, I chased you, remember."

"Oh yeah, well it took charm to keep you." Ms. Allerton stopped in front of us, never once casting a glance at Russell or myself whose arms she held onto. Risha gave her a kiss on her cheek.

"Momma I'd like to introduce you to Brian Marshall and his brother Russell."

"Which one is the groom, dear?" She pulled me closer to herself,

"This one's mine."

"Well thank God for small miracles," her mother said loud enough to hear. Russell didn't seem to catch the remark. This was going to take determination but I was adamant about putting my best face forward and keeping it there. I put on a cheesy smile, stuck out my hand and greeted her.

"Hello Ms. Allerton, I've been looking forward to meeting you."

"I'll bet," she remarked, ignoring my outstretched hand. I withdrew it but kept up the front.

"You have a great daughter, so that would make you a great mother."

"I'm well aware of that, just ask me what's on your mind."

Ms. Allerton, I love your daughter very much and I'd like to ask for your blessings on our becoming man and wife."

"Brian honey, before I give you my blessings, did you and my daughter discuss in depth all of the details concerning this union?"

"Well, we haven't gone over too much yet but trust me we're ready for a life together. Everything else will work itself out."

"Everything will not work itself out and knowing my daughter, she has not discussed the most important thing with you."

"May I ask what you're referring to?" She was wearing me out and my changing vibe was apparent. Risha who hadn't spoken a word up until now squeezed my arm extra hard.

"MOM," She said in a warning tone. With no hint of acknowledgement she heard her daughter, Ms. Allerton continued.

"Well Brian, it would really mean a great deal to us if you would be considerate enough to agree to a prenuptial, you know just in case."

"Excuse me! Just in case what?"

"How well does Risha really know you? She's going into this whole marriage thing leading with her heart so I have to be the one to watch the pocketbook. Even you should understand she has a lot to lose if you bail after the first year, whereas you have everything to gain."

"MOTHER, I asked you not to show out!"

"Look Risha, I only said what you should have been thinking. Besides, it's my job to protect you from all the wolves out there you see and those that are dressed in sheep's clothing. Trust me, you'll thank me later." I remained silent.

It would be better for both of us if Risha finished this conversation with her mother.

"You know what I was thinking Mama, when we do get married which we are with no strings attached, Brian as my other half will have complete access to the finances. As the man of the house he will have the say so as to whether you get cut off or not. If YOU do not want to be poor again, I suggest you cut the harassment and accept your future son in law with blessings."

"Well, I see this was not the proper time to discuss the dimensions of your relationship," Ms. Allerton smiled.

"Discussions about me and Brian are permanently closed Mother."

"Well then, I guess I have no choice but to give you two my blessings."

"Thank you." Things went much better when my parents sauntered over to where we were standing. The two women hit it off with like minds of all things women find interesting and men don't. Mother praised Ms. Allerton as being the quintessential host. If I hadn't been the recipient of Ms. Allerton's bipolar view of our classes, I would have agreed with Mama. Russell remained quiet most of the evening except for a polite thank you here and there. I wondered when his need for a fix would start hounding him but I didn't inquire. If I don't mention it, he won't think about it, I hope. Risha gave those that requested it, a walking tour of the house. I was next to her holding hands but I was a sightseer as well. My baby spoke enthusiastically as she described in great detail the history of the house and how we were going to do a little history making ourselves. I couldn't help but feel a little uneasy about Risha and myself. Contrary to Risha's attempt at hiding her truth from me, the clues were still there. I had to agree with Ms. Allerton in one respect, I called myself knowing her and now I felt like I really didn't. I guess I was blinded by a new love. Whatever the reason my eyes are open from now on.

"Brian, Brian honey, Risha was pulling on me. You okay?"

"Yea, I'm sorry. You were asking me something."

"Yes, let's disappear. I need a moment."

"Lead the way."

"RISHAA!"

Then there was Mama. It was obvious to all Mama approved of my choice, although I think the fame and fortune had a lot to do with it. She never bothered to have that woman-to-woman conversation with Risha, instead speaking only of her character on the show.

"Yes Mrs. Marshall," Risha answered as Mama pulled her away from me.

...ONE WEEK BEFORE
THE WEDDING...

THE SILENT BUZZ of the message alert startled Risha as it did every other time it went off. One quick read and she was upset.

>Hey Beautiful, Your Mandingo warrior is in town. I've forgiven you so It's time to make up. Hit me back<

"Shit, why the hell can't he understand?" She had too many things to do today and entertaining an abusive ex was not on her list. She ignored the text and went about her business. One hour later her cellphone rings showing the callers Id as Imperitus. One press of the ignore button afforded her more temporary solitude. In the middle of shopping she made a beeline to her car where Dale was waiting.

"Dale, do you remember Imperitus?"

"Yes Ms. Allerton, I remember him." Dale never forgot a fool and Imperitus was a fool times two. He was a big sonofabitch, played for Tampa Bay, Defensive line he believed. Talk about black and ugly, and about as smart as a rock.

"He's been trying to reach me and I've been ignoring his calls." Dale could hear the nervousness in her voice and for good reason. The last straw of their one and a half year relationship climaxed with a drunken Imperitus attacking Risha in the shower. He had appeared at her home that morning after being gone for three days on one of his usual binges. Her only advantage was he was so drunk he could not get a good hold on the slippery woman. He resorted to punching with the hopes of stopping or at least slowing her down a bit so he could have his way. Grazing her more than once, she dodged and executed acrobatic maneuvers over furniture determined on staying out of his reach. He was a powerful man and every glancing blow produced a sizeable bruise. Imperitus stayed in front of her using his football skills to effectively cut down her running room with the help of furniture being used to block exits. She tried to make it to the front door, it being the only way out and help from Dale but a final lunge stopped her a foot short of freedom. She could do nothing but wait for his next move since the crushing weight of his body rendered her immobile. She felt like a mouse caught by the cat whose every indication was to do her great harm.

"Let's have some fun," he grunted while he pawed at her naked body. In a desperate attempt not to be raped, Risha sank her teeth into anything flesh, not stopping until the taste of blood was fresh on her tongue. Imperitus rolled off of her, his concern for the painful wound a more pressing matter at the moment. The diversion gave her the time she needed to bolt out the front door screaming for help as she ran towards Dale. Dale's practiced response was swift as he ran around to the passenger side and opened the door but by the time he put the car in drive, Imperitus was in the back seat. Risha was not giving in no matter what and with energy renewed she fought back yet again. Imperitus punched the terrified woman in the side then pinned her arms with one hand as he positioned himself to take what was his. Dale dreaded getting involved but knew there was no other way around it. He rolled the partition down. Imperitus looked up at him quizzically.

"Roll that fucking window up Dale, This ain't no show." Risha was sobbing as she prayed Dale finally grew a pair of balls. Dale had been through this scene with these two many times before and as he had tried to tell Risha more than once, the man means her no good. Now in broad daylight with him as a witness, he is going to rape her in the car. What's next, murder? He had thought about his own daughter and what must be done.

"Sir, I'm about twenty years older than you and over a hundred pounds lighter but I am not going to sit here and watch you hurt Ms. Allerton anymore."

"You want to stop me old man."

"If I have to I will, until the police get here.

"The police, you called the police? I don't hear anything.

"Listen." The far off sounds of sirens broke the silence in the car changing Imperitus's cruel approach to one of gentleness.

"Damn baby, I fucked up again. I promise I'll be good from now on. Here, Imperitus dug in his pockets, pulled out a wad of bills and dropped them onto Risha's lap. This is my gift to you, now let's go back in our house and forget I acted like such an ass." He pulled on her arm expecting no protest but this time she held firm. Risha was through with the relationship months ago but the attention she received from being with a star football player superseded the abusive treatment from his drunken outbursts. It was an eighteen-month learning curve she had to endure to begin putting herself first. Lesson learned, she was through. She spoke, emboldened by the back up speeding closer to their destination.

"That's my house, not yours. All traces of you will be on the front lawn for garbage pickup today. You can keep the keys because they'll be worthless in the next hour or so. When the police get here, I am going to press charges against you and take it all the way to having you put in jail. Once I'm done with you, the only football playing you'll be doing is for the prison. My last words to you are, disappear before the police get here and they sound pretty close." Imperitus squeezed her neck and snarled about seeing her the next time he was back in town. He got into his car and sped off only to get picked up two blocks away for speeding and running a stop sign. Dale hadn't seen him since and never asked what became of her threat to him. He had informed Risha if she chose any more fools, he would have to resign. His heart couldn't take but so much.

"So what do you want to do Ms. Allerton?"

"I don't know. I don't want to tell Brian, he'll kill him and wind up in jail because of me." Dale laughed.

"Ms. Allerton, I doubt if Brian is a match for Imperitus."

"You haven't seen him fight. Trust me, he could put Imperitus down easily."

"Even if that's so, you said you're not going to tell him." As if on cue, her cell phone buzzed.

"Imperitus?"

"Yea, it's him again. Risha sat halfway in the car and started typing.

"There, she swung her legs in and closed the door. Let's go." Bewildered, Dale put the car in drive.

"Where are we headed?" Ms. Allerton.

"Oh I'm sorry, the police station. I told him to meet us there where I will have him charged with attempted rape. I also told him if I don't see him, to be sure to have a rotten life. I bet he don't show up. Risha jumped, startled from the sudden vibration of the phone."

>Fuck-U-Bitch< Risha showed the text to Dale. He nodded approvingly.

"Okay where were we, oh yes, I hear Lord and Taylors calling my name."

...WEDDING BELLS...

I ARRIVED AT THE Royal Oaks at exactly one P.M. A large round stage stood complete with more than a hundred white balloons attached around the perimeter with a double row forming a path from the two different directions we were going to march in from. An empty podium and behind it a giant big screen T.V. stood silent waiting for the ceremony to begin. Guests arrived hours ahead of time, each vying for a seat as close as possible. Immediate family members and special invitees had reserved seats so there was no need for them to be so early. When we started planning this wedding Risha had so many girlfriends that wanted to be a part of it, they drew straws to see who was in and who was out. I had Russell spend the night at my apartment so there wouldn't be any problems getting him here. Other than his need for dope the evening was uneventful. Once we, I paid, he copped, he nodded himself right into a good nights sleep. Risha also hit me up the same evening to go over a few details with me. Her show decided our event would be advantageous to use as a ratings boost. Instead of a private affair it will be televised to entice more viewers to the show. Everything was being taken care of by them including our honeymoon destination, which would be kept secret. Fans were going to be there alongside news people from the rags and the network. She warned of the bad fans or haters who seem to make it their business to create a disturbance in the name of getting even with the character. They think the characters portrayed are real. The admirers are sometimes a problem also because their love for the character can be fanatical. Their claim to fame is to get a souvenir by any means necessary.

I looked at my watch for the hundredth time following the second hand around its circumference repeatedly counting the numbers off in my head. So far we were approaching one hour behind schedule with no end in sight. My stomach, which was fine yesterday was knotted up today. One of the groomsmen who I grew up with came over to sooth me. He slipped a little pink pill into my hand.

"It's chewable and you look like you need it. Your brother doesn't look so good either but I can't help him." The speaker system crackled. Gentlemen five minutes until the march. Okay this is it. I sat next to Russell to see what I could do. He was shaking like he had the flu.

"You think you can make it, Russell, I asked with serious doubt." I had made him promise me he would not get high today but now I wasn't so sure that was the right choice.

"Nah man, I'm sick. I need a little something to take the edge off until I can cop."

"Shit Russell, you know I don't have anything. Can't you hold it in until after the ceremony?"

-Street 101- when a junkie is kicking first thing to come up is everything in his stomach.

"Yea, Fuck it let's go." The door opened and two by two they stomped in tune to a jazzed up version of here comes the bride. Russell threw up behind the door, wiped his mouth and somehow dragged his ravaged body on to pair with the maid of honor. I saw her grimace as they tried to stomp in step. Russell had his handkerchief up to his mouth in a last ditch effort to keep in what wanted to come out. After they were all in place I started my dance. A sea of people stood from the door to the stage. I followed their course to a drumbeat that picked up speed as I got closer. A man's booming voice could be heard talking to me in reference to the last mile. The raised floor lit up with each step as I moved closer toward the stage. My final fifty yards was over a bridge that sported a koi pond underneath where the drums became thunderous. At the end I took my spot inside the semicircle made up of my groomsmen. The music stopped and silence was demanded of the crowd. The same deep voiced speaker announced the coming of the bride better known as Risha Allerton. The roar of engines signaled the passing of a small twin-engine plane overhead. LOOK UP, his voice boomed, AND SEE THE MAGIC OF TRUE LOVE. We looked up to see a bright red banner following the plane that read-- TODAY RISHA ALLERTON WILL BE WED TO THE LOVE OF HER LIFE--BRIAN MARSHALL. Hundreds of small favors floated down to earth each attached to a tiny parachute. Russell elbowed me claiming I was one lucky son of a bitch. I agreed with him before he excused himself heaving as he exited. We no sooner lost sight of the plane, when the whirling blades of a helicopter made itself known. The pearly white helicopter descended on a selected spot on the lawn not fifty feet from us. Two half naked bodybuilders jogged to the door carrying a rolled up red carpet. In unison they flung it in the direction of where we were, it unraveling to its end at the front of the steps. The two body builders knelt on either side of the door and waited. First to exit were two children, each carrying a basket of different colored roses. They danced along the side of the carpet path distributing flowers.

Faint music wafted on the breeze. As the seconds passed the music grew louder until two full blown marching bands appeared battling it out as they marched around the stage. Pop exited looking handsome in his white Tux and once again you could hear a pin drop as he helped Risha out onto the carpet. The two young children completed their task and took their place next to the maid of honor. My lady was pulling out all the stops in order to grab the imaginations of all who viewed this event. I had to admit, my baby looked fantastic in the hottest wedding dress I'd ever seen. For the past week she had entertained various designers who wanted her to wear their creations for all the world to see. Her make up artist was none other than Mauricio Encarlo. There wasn't a famous face he hadn't put his magic touch on. I heard, since I wasn't allowed to be there that, Risha was escorted via a white Bentley to his Estate where a team of makeup artists and hairdressers descended on her at his command. He directed them as a coach would in a big game, not leaving anything up to anyone else's imagination. His creative power and his staff's expertise combined to make her a Goddess. A thunderous cheer went up as she curtsied and both bands Jazzed it up as she and my father did their thing on the carpet. Risha tripped as she took the last step to be my side. Without thought I caught her before she hit the floor and lifted her upright. She kissed me as I gently placed her back on her feet. The crowd went wild.

"Was that fall planned," I asked while we waited for the pastor to finish praying.

"Of course husband to be, it's all planned down to the last letter."

"How did you know I would catch you?"

"You got my back, right?"

"You carrying this back thing a little far."

"I know you. You were watching my every move and as fast as I know you are, I wasn't worried."

"You are such a hound."

"Yes I am," she said, pleased with herself. The famous minister who I was in awe of and who had presided over our pre marital counseling stepped to the podium.

"Are you two ready," he asked with the gentleness of a man talking to his own children.

"Yes Grandfather." My mouth dropped as I mouthed the words, Grandfather?

"Take her hand and let's begin."

Right after the ceremony, Russell was dropped off in his neighborhood with at his request one thousand dollars. Paying him off was fine with me, I looked at it as payment for you to go your way and I go mine. Dealing with him and his drug problem was not for me and besides he was not the same brother I knew growing up. Mama later gave me the, I told you so's while Pop remained his usual thoughtful quiet self. You can't say I didn't try.

Wouldn't you know the following day the first page picture in one paper that was as large as the paper itself was not any of the fashion or beauty of the wedding. No, it had to be the moment I opened my mouth in genuine surprise when I learned about the pastor being my brides Grandfather. It was a small and trivial private moment but the headlines above the picture read in big bold type:

>Hubby to be gets the surprise of his life< (in smaller words), >God only knows what secrets she imparts to him minutes before they are to be wed< You would think this was one of those rag magazines, not a nationally known newspaper. I was glad the rest of the papers didn't go that route. One paper read > A TRUE KNIGHT IN A TUX < Brian Marshall who until recently was unknown to the entertainment community showed with amazing speed that love has no boundaries. The former Ms. Allerton had a potentially disastrous fall only to be caught at the last possible moment by none other than her ever-vigilant fiancé. Risha reminded me not to get too caught up in too much media rhetoric. After what I'd seen already, it seemed best to follow that advice. We went on our honeymoon with the accompaniment of the media. Photographers with super telescopic lenses tried to get a shot of anything interesting, especially brown skin. It wasn't long before they got tired of chasing us around, as Risha wasn't in that circle of stars yet for reporters to waste much time and money on.

We returned on a stormy Wednesday late in the afternoon. The only one to meet us this time was Dale. Our stay out of the country lasted longer than what we intended because Risha insisted she needed more time. Since the choice of destinations was my pick I decided for out of the ordinary. Africa seemed the best bet for a young man who had never traveled before. At first Risha felt it would not be like a honeymoon. The French Riviera or Cozumel she argued was a better bet, somewhere known for newlywed getaways where we would be wined and catered to, not Africa. With a little mild persuasion and a friendly yet unbreakable bet she relented. If she didn't like it after the first day she gets to choose a different destination and we leave immediately. If she likes it, I receive sex from her when and where at a second's notice, no questions asked. After payment she laughed "I never lost a better bet in my life, silly man." We stayed an extra three weeks.

...LIVING, LOVING, SNAG...

RISHA'S FAME INCREASED, along with her work schedule as she predicted but her prolonged absenteeism increased as well. We were no longer the inseparable couple everyone knew us to be. When taping time began for new episodes, twelve to fourteen hour days would be the norm for about six months. Now she turns around and becomes involved in a movie project part of which takes place in another country. I try to understand for the sake of our happiness but in dealing with emotions sometimes the choice is already made by the subconscious. It starts out as an inconspicuous erosion, like a mosquito bite you didn't realize was there until it started itching. Over time that tiny thing builds on itself, adding other tiny things so you never know the original cause. You start counting the days you haven't seen your wife. You eat alone most nights now. She calls and you put up a believable front, maybe that's a mistake because it gives her the peace of mind that whenever she's available, you'll be there waiting. She comes home and you two can't get enough of each other. The bed gets a well-needed workout and you are inseparable once again. You start feeling like your old self because she's around, but in no time at all she's gone again and it's not like you didn't know, you were told she only had three days then off to finish shooting in Spain.

"You want to come?" she asked and I declined. Tried it once and it was worse than being home alone. Now I'm upset again because I was too happy to think about sitting her down to explain the loneliness I felt when we're apart.

About this time, Russell also began making himself a nuisance. The knowledge of my marrying into money became his second addiction. I explained that money was not what he needed and he'd hang up only to call back again.

"I'm in a life and death situation here," he said. He was more akin to an animal in the wild than a human being. Basic needs dictated his every move, with me being part of newly acquired knowledge of a money source. I had asked him what changed since we started communicating that now he can't do without my help.

"I just need you," was his answer. My answer to that was for him to do what he'd been doing when I wasn't around. Again I got a hang up.

Before I left my job Risha's viewing audience there increased two fold. She had become the topic of many discussions. Some included me getting an autographed picture for everybody, but most conversations were behind my back.

"Monique is some kinda' bitch," one co-worker commented as I walked into the lounge. That's all I heard because all three female co-workers became quiet as soon as my presence was known. I had never given it much thought but now thinking about it piqued my interest, so one lonely night I made it my business to set my TiVo up. Next evening, the boring music at the show's beginning turned me off and the fear of seeing something I don't want to see. Either way it would be several more months before I forced myself to watch it.

Several Months Later

HOW BAD COULD it be, I thought. It was daytime soap for god's sake. If I can't deal with her character on TV, Lord knows what I'm going to feel seeing her on the big screen. I kept an open mind, secure in the knowledge this was make pretend, nothing more. As the show began it didn't take long for Risha to pop up. I sat mesmerized while Monique seduced another woman's CEO husband in a successful attempt to sleep with him. After the deed was done, a video copy from a camera she had secreted in the ceiling of her bedroom was sent to his office and so began the extortion of thousands of dollars from him. I got hooked watching this person who acted so believably well, it made me second guess what was real and what was fake. I didn't have the nerve to tell her, she was being tested from time to time only because of me looking at her show and having doubts about her chaste. My jealousy that I thought was under control had been laying dormant, waiting for any chance to pop back up.

…ANOTHER DAY IN CRESTON LAKE…

"SO THOMAS, IF you don't have plans for the evening, I know a quaint spot we could be alone together."

"Should I ask what type of business we would be conducting there?"

"The type most of you young, handsome males like with a beautiful black woman."

"Sounds like an offer I can't refuse, let me call my wife and postpone our dinner plans, looks like I'll be putting in a little overtime."

"Good, I'll meet you there. Can't have the hired help catch wind of our little get together or they might run and tell wifey."

"A commercial break, it could not have come at a better time." I closed my eyes and put my head back for a few seconds, then went to fix myself a cup of coffee. I'd decided I had seen enough but the commercials were finished when I got back and Monique was in the hotel room pulling at Thomas's clothes and kissing him all over the lips. I aimed the remote at the screen but pushing the button to another channel was impossible as long as she was on the screen. My baby slowly sank down out of camera shot looking up at him with a wicked grin I had never seen before. It was easy to tell his hands were on her head while he stood there with that look all men have when their dick is in a woman's mouth. They transition into the bedroom hand in hand where the real dirt went down. He is on top and his hands are roaming over every part of her body as he made sure he got familiar with my baby. Wait a minute, was that a slip of the sheet the crew didn't notice. Did I see his penis disappear inside my wife? Are they really fucking under those sheets? TIVO got a workout that would've voided its warranty if they had known replay and slow motion was used repeatedly for two hours. As much as I tried, there was never any real definitive clarity one way or another. The station got a call from me needing to talk to someone in charge.

Two rings, four rings, six rings, no answer. I'm beside myself with my hunger for answers. The cellphone rings, it's answered before the first ring is finished. I don't wait for a greeting, I need to know when she is coming home. She hears it in my voice and now she's alarmed and tells me she's on her way. My wife's beautiful face had ended the show with her lips sealed on his. The emotional strain this show was putting on me was too much. I needed some reassurance from her and the show itself about all this sex stuff and showing your body on TV. Risha came through the door in record time rushing to my side. I had calmed myself down waiting for her arrival but after that entrance all control was lost.

"I SAW YOU FUCKING SOME WHITE GUY ON TV. HOW COULD THEY ALLOW THAT AND WHY WOULD YOU DO THAT TO ME? YOU LET HIM STICK HIS TONGUE DOWN YOUR THROAT, HE RUBBED HIS FUCKING HANDS ALL OVER YOU AND YOU TOOK OFF YOUR CLOTHES. My voice cracked on the words and tears started to flow, I saw it all," I said. I could feel my anxiety heighten to a degree I had never known in all my life.

"BRIAN, BRIAN, CALM DOWN, calm down honey. Listen to yourself." Risha put her hands on my cheeks. The sweet scent of her perfume wafted through me as I looked into warm and inviting eyes. I struggled to regain my composure somewhat, enough to at least listen.

"Baby, it's a show and in a show we act. If I wanted any of those men you see, I would not have married you."

"But you were naked in the bed. He was on top of you. I saw…

"You saw a body suit. Not only would I not be naked on TV, the FCC would fine us and probably shut us down for an X rated performance on daytime TV.

"That looked pretty close to X from where I sat."

"Yeah, the writer's like to push the envelope a little."

"A little?

-You kissed him."

"Yes, that I did. It's a part of the script, it doesn't mean a thing."

"I'll bet when he stuck his tongue down your throat it meant something to him."

"Brian your imagination is getting the best of you. I don't stick my tongue in nobody else's mouth except my husband. She casually kissed me, simultaneously sliding her tongue past my lips. UMMM, there husband of mine, only you receive the wife's treatment. You are my husband, right?" She was right about that but I still did not want to share her.

"Yes I am," I replied a little too timidly."

"Anything else husband of mine."

"Well one thing," I whispered in her ear. She patted my crotch.

"Good idea." She led me into the bedroom. A week later I looked at another steamy scene this time with a woman.

"DAMN, don't they have any one else on this soap that can be a bitch for a while."

...TWO YEARS MARRIED...

"MRS. ALLERTON, COME quick," the receptionist, whispered as loud as possible across the set where the cast was taping. The director glared at her with annoyance but said nothing other than cut. Risha rushed outside to find me in an argument with security.

"I told you who I was and if you touch me again I'm going to kick your ass." Before Risha could intervene both security guards put their hands on me in a vain attempt at preventing me from entering the set. I rear headed one in the nose and grabbed the others hand twisting it in such a vicious manner it broke. Ten seconds was all it took, as neither man was in any kind of shape for a fight.

"BRIAN, WHAT ARE YOU DOING HERE?" I hadn't seen Risha standing there with her face twisted into a frown.

"We got to get some things cleared up," I did not care about the costs of my disruption beyond my own satisfaction since that was by far more important. Risha was not intimidated like the rest of the coworkers were. Her voice shook with emotion as she told me to go home. I left without another word.

Risha did not come home that night, nor did she call. I stayed up for what seemed like hours waiting to hear the door open so we could finish this. A snap decision was made to visit her haunts in the off chance she's been seen and if not then to pass my card around, asking for a call if she appears. Not knowing what to do after I'd been everywhere I could think of, home was my next stop until a brilliant thought comes to mind and I make a hard U-turn in the direction of that actors house, Frank something or other Risha claimed was just a colleague. Who else could comfort her on a moment's notice that she trusts and would understand? Her girlfriends might be able to but he was already there, I'm sure jumping at this opportunity to console her. I wouldn't be surprised if it was he who invited my Risha to chill at his place for a while to calm down. I knew his address, having acquired that information months ago, for just in case reasons. Right now it is a certainty in my mind that she went to be consoled by her good male friend. He works with her daily, which makes them pretty knowledgeable about each other including his touching her as I have. Risha claims they use body suits when they are fake fucking but she cannot tell me that she doesn't feel an erection when he is rubbing up against her. How many orgasms has he had in the name of acting, I wondered? The sight of those two together now was as clear in my head as the first episode I watched of their infidelity together.

He ushers her into his home, thanking God with every fiber of his being that he was at work today. All that make believe sex on the set was an overture to what the reality was to be at last, now that she was in his home. An actor first, he plays his best role yet, a gentleman, friend and colleague listening with an attentive ear, words of support ready to be spoken at the perfect time. Trophies litter the house in the way of trinkets, items confiscated from other needy female souls to feed a super big ego. He talks like a friend to a friend, meeting emotional needs one by one to break down a barrier already weakened. His crime is one that most men from another color have, a sweet tooth. It's that need to taste the ultimate in chocolate at any cost. He leads her to his magnificent plush couch, luxurious in feel, meant for relaxation amidst other hidden pleasures. As she sits, he takes the liberty of removing her shoes, enabling tired feet to be massaged as they are lifted up to attain a more comfortable resting position. He's enjoying the feel of soft black flesh, remembering the show and how much he craved her then. He thinks she'll probably be a wild woman in his bed because of her need to release, which only serves to make him more anxious, more hopeful. He tells her he will kiss her troubles away, make her forget at least for a moment all the shit I'm putting her through. She puts up a mild front but she's weak and he knows it. He's inches from her lips, so close he can feel her cool breath on her face. Her eyes are closed with eyelids still damp from evaporating tears he wishes to kiss but he refrains. There is a bigger prize to take possession of. His lips touch hers ever so lightly, she pulls back but not much. He tells her it's okay, pulling her to him instead and this time she doesn't pull back. Hers is an overwhelming need to be, at this moment loved. He doesn't waste a second, afraid he could lose her at any time from guilt. He disrobes her all the while talking to her, caressing her. They are in the bedroom now and I step on the gas. My intention is to catch those two in the act. A vigorous headshake gets my reasonable side to start cursing me out. What's wrong with you fool, you know damn well that woman loves you. She would do nothing to hurt you, especially what you're thinking about, yet you disrespect her with all your jealous antics. She would more likely be at some girlfriend's house cooling down. Better bet is her mother but then again Risha knows if her mother had the slightest notion

I drove her daughter out into the streets she would go to great lengths to break us up no matter the cost. Go home Brian and wait, I say out loud.

The Actor's estate loomed in sight and I figured, what harm could it do to see if he at least knew where she might be? I rang the bell at the gate and on hearing my name, was granted entry. When I saw the handsome man at the door in real life, my reasonable side changed colors. He had this cocky air about him I hated right off. He stood about six two, which surprised me. I heard most of the so-called good looking actors were short in real life. This dude was the whole package. He was a physical specimen with a tanned surfer type body, chiseled face and baby blue eyes. I demanded to speak with my wife.

"Risha? Why would she be here?" Jesus, he talks like he's acting.

"Then you won't mind my checking for myself." I pushed my way in and started looking for the bedroom, which in a house the size of Manhattan wasn't easy. The damn place was beautiful too, right out of a magazine. If I were to guess, It boasted a Mediterranean type design with the huge white marble pillars on either side of the entry way, statues on stands of naked white people posing with missing hands and feet carefully placed in various corners and looking up were alternating low to high hung Tiffany chandeliers lighting the way over a winding matching marble staircase to the upstairs rooms.

"ARE YOU OUT OF YOUR FUCKING MIND, GET THE HELL OUT OF MY HOUSE." He's talking to someone on the phone, but I don't care, I know she's here. Frank follows me upstairs yelling all the way which is ignored until he does something stupid. The poker he strikes me with hurts like hell but not enough to stop me where I couldn't defend myself. I kicked him into one of those naked female statues positioned at the top of the stairs and began beating him with my fists demanding to see my wife. I draw blood but he doesn't give her up. The police arrive with guns drawn, ordering me to lie on the ground. Where the hell is Risha? I know she heard all the noise we were making, and yet she doesn't come to my aid. Fucking bitch, we're going to get to the bottom of this when I catch up to her.

Twenty-four hours. That's how long I'm held until Frank, feeling more sympathy than anything else drops the charges. He does take out a restraining order though. That in my eyes solidified the truth I knew all along. All the stress this woman was putting me through was wearing me down to the point where something's got to give. A search of the house for any signs of her presence since my forced lock down turned into an all out furniture flying, door kicking, energy wasting affair. Fifteen minutes and twenty or thirty thousand dollars worth of damage later I was rummaging through her personal effects for numbers, letters anything with a name and a way of speaking with someone. I then got on the phone and called any and everyone with a name and number attached to it. I started out very charming as I tried to entice her stuck up friends to reveal her whereabouts. After the third unsuccessful call my charm changed to bluntness in my quest for answers. When her male friends were asked and she had many, some had the nerve to threaten me with informing Risha of my cloak and dagger issues. Already at my breaking point, I shouted into the tiny cell phone real threats of beating someone down. The intensity of a door slamming shut vibrated through the walls. I stepped into the front room prepared for an argument and stopped in my tracks at her sight. Risha stood there stunned, mascara tears streaming down her beautiful face that another man had been kissing on.

"Where the hell have you been?" I moved in her direction, stopping short of an overturned Tiffany pole lamp that one hour ago had stood majestic in all its crystalline glory. She didn't flinch. Her jawline was tight from exertion as her eyes stayed locked in on mine. Grabbing her by the arms, I was determined to get some answers.

"You were asked a question."

"So you going to beat me for answers now, Brian?"

"You still didn't answer my question which tells me…"

"Tells you what! What the hell does it tell you Brian?"

"That you trying to think up a good lie, but you can't fool me."

"OH MY GOD, REALLY? AGAIN WE HAVE TO GO THROUGH THIS NO TRUSTING ME SHIT. YOU ARE OUT OF YOUR FUCKING MIND AND YOU'RE TRYING TO TAKE ME THERE WITH YOU. Risha pushed me aside and headed towards the bedroom kicking broken furniture out of her way as she shook her head.

"You need help," she declared as she disappeared into the room. I sat down amongst the mess I made trying to sort out what was going on in my head. I used my t-shirt to wipe the spit I didn't have the nerve to touch while she screamed at me. None of my questions were answered, yet now I felt I was the guilty party. What a change in events. With colors back to normal, my reasonable side said, I told you so.

The ringing sound of her phone from the bedroom caused my heart to skip a beat. Damn, round two, I thought as my stomach rolled over in agreement. A few muffled words, a sincere apologetic exchange from her and then nothing. She's thinking right now and that scares me. The biggest decisions right or wrong are made in these scant moments. Risha appeared in the doorway of the bedroom her face a mass of concentrated lines formed from the stress of problems stacking up out of control.

"You went to my fellow colleague's house."

"Let me explain." Risha held up a hand.

"No, I'm still trying to grasp the fact that you literally had the nerve to go to Frank's house looking for me. Do you want me laughed right out of the business, is that what you want? Risha's stance suggested she was about to fly across the room and knock the hell out of me but instead she took a deep breath and continued. You know you missed out on all of the other men and women I slept with throughout my time on the show. Do you need their names and addresses as well or do you already have them?" I couldn't possibly tell her I probably had most of her contacts and used them. I prayed her phone would stay silent the rest of the night, at least until she calmed down a little,

"LOOK, Risha stated with a finality in her voice. THIS IS YOUR LAST CHANCE BRIAN, I can't live like this. You are not going to kill me over your jealous bullshit. Get a therapist, find out what the hell is wrong and FIX IT or honey, WE ARE DONE." She made her way through the mess flinging items this way and that until she was at the front door. She slammed it so hard I could swear a window broke in one of the other rooms. I cursed myself out repeatedly for being such an ass. I got busy cleaning up as best as I could and managed to fix her a good meal in the interim. Food always seems to calm the savage beast, in this case the very angry wife. The meal worked along with a thousand apologies and a promise that in the morning I would seek out a shrink. She was at her mother's house all along.

...THREE YEARS MARRIED...

SOME MONTHS WERE good, some not so good, it went in waves. My therapist laid out a plan for me to follow in the hopes of my gaining the emotional stability needed to deal with her career and my issues. Look at yourself in the mirror and repeat your mantra everyday, she said. If you find yourself getting angry with your wife for reasons you don't quite understand, take a walk, breath in some fresh air, enjoy the scenery, take in a movie. Mingle with other people on your own, be the life of the party. Do something other than sitting and letting your imagination create a destructive illusion. Always remember to talk to your wife and not at her. She is not your pet.

I heard the music coming from the bedroom when I stepped through the door.

Not a good sign. I had avoided Risha like the plague lately and though I loved her dearly, sharing her and all the intimate things she did in her role with men and women alike was something I found impossible to get over. She refused to give up her role as Monique' who I felt was the source of all our troubles. Since being with me, Risha had developed this need to display her emotional state of the moment by playing different types of music. I knew it was more my fault than hers for our relationship to be so strained but I didn't know what else to do. I intended to work out a solution soon but soon was always another time. I did almost everything the therapist suggested. Talking to Risha about us wasn't one of them. No matter what, I think I'm progressing. No more tantrums and the new furniture is still intact. Drinking at the bar became a good fit as opposed to sitting in front of the TV getting sick to my stomach. The music was sad and non-forgiving and although it was one of my favorite songs, tonight it would represent one of the most painful moments in our marriage.

"Risha, I called out, is everything all right Honey?" I knew full well this was not the case but I had to hope otherwise. Risha was in the kitchen scrubbing the floors. Bad sign number two. She had this tendency to thoroughly clean while the sad music played. This helped her to organize her thoughts on what issues to complain to me about. Lately the sad music had been playing frequently, which for me meant that I stay away for longer periods of time. Tonight, I came home early with the intentions of surprising her with flowers and a card. It was time I got us back on track and besides, I was horny. I looked forward to the make up sex part that was always a mind blower. Risha turned to me with a look that all men knew, no matter what is said or done this wasn't going to be a good night. I tepidly held up the dozen red roses and the card to which both were ignored. She walked past me into the living room, her staging area for our final battle. I followed her like a lost child not knowing which way she was going.

"You know Brian," she turned to face me. Risha looked at me searching for the courage to say the two words that would turn the evening into the worst day of my young life.

"It's over."

"It's over?"

"Yes, it's over." I was what you might call shell shocked. No argument, no crying, no lashing out. We both stood there not more than three feet apart. Her arms were folded under those thirty eight C braless breasts straining against a one size too small Tee shirt that was wet from all the cleaning she was doing. Her short shorts would have shown most of what she was endowed with if not for her black panties covering up what the shorts missed. Any other day this scene would have been enough to make me carry her off to the bedroom but right now that thought was the farthest thing from my mind. You'd be able to hear a pin drop if not for that sad ass music playing in the backroom.

"What selection is this one?" I thought.

"Don't you have anything to say Brian? I said I'm leaving you.

-Well SAY something!" I had a thousand things to say but it's hard getting past the numbness that envelopes you and constricts your thoughts.

"I can't think right now, can you give me some time."

"Wow, I'm sorry Brian, your time is up."

"Baby, whatever it is we can fix it," I pushed those words out in desperation.

"You know and I know that 'WE' can't be fixed. You are a child in a man's body and I can't stick around wondering when you are going to grow up. What did you think was going to eventually happen? I warned you over and over again and you just brushed it off. I thought I picked the right man by stepping out of my social arena but I see I was wrong. There are a few real men waiting on the sidelines for our marriage to end and although I struck them all down before, I sure am game for them now. At the very least Brian you will be a rich man after our divorce is final and my advice to you is look in the mirror and change the ugly side of your personality. You won't stand a chance in this world if you don't."

"I don't want a divorce."

"I know you don't and honestly neither do I, but I have to. My career, my health, and my sanity are all at stake here. I need all of those things to function properly and you're slowly eroding each and every one of them."

"I know I can be a real ass at times, but that comes from falling so deeply in love with you. I've never felt like this before nor will I ever feel this way again. I truly do not want anybody else in my life."

"You'll feel that way again, it takes time to heal. Risha in a moment of calm took my hands and sat down with me. Look Baby, don't think I don't love you with all my heart but our timing for each other is off. I didn't think about your feelings when it came to what I wanted, which truth be told was selfish on my part. I know you were compelled into being jealous because you're lonely and what I do for a living is one of your Achilles heels probably because you seldom see me except on TV and then your only focus is on me being intimate with someone else instead of being here more often with you. I expected you to be okay with being alone for long periods of time while I worked or attended the hundreds of functions necessary to keep the show's ratings up. Our worlds our vastly different, but I thought that with love and understanding and communication we could possibly fuse the two into one. Now I have serious doubts about everything.

-I shouldn't have married you so soon. I think if we had taken it a little slower and grew into each other, things would have been easier to handle on both our parts."

"So, then we need to try harder."

"I don't know Brian, I have a big problem with you disappearing every night to everywhere but here. Or stalking my every move thinking you're invisible. We wouldn't ever have had this talk if I never spoke up. When I am home, I expect you to be at least horny enough to want some sex.

-So where were you all those nights you weren't in our bed?" Risha's tone grew stern again as she folded her arms in anticipation of my answer. I always hated these sudden on the spot questions.

"I just hung out, I answered. I closed a lot of places and I saw a lot of movies. Sometimes I stayed at a hotel."

"Anything to not be around me, huh."

"I was angry with you."

"That's a lot of anger."

"Yea, I guess."

"You don't think that's a little extreme."

"I didn't at the moment but in retrospect, yea, I guess it was a little."

"About your hotel stays, you didn't tell me if you were alone or if you were being relieved of your anger."

"I'm married, why would I do that?"

"Married, don't stop an erection on no man when they stray. We both know you like sex as much as you like eating. And you damn sure wasn't fucking me."

"Well, I didn't."

"Okay." Risha got up off of the couch.

"I know you don't believe me but I'm not lying."

"I never said I don't believe you, as a matter of fact, I do. You going there at all is what pisses me off. Is it really that hard to just talk to me?"

"Sometimes."

"Well I suggest you speak now because your marriage depends on it."

"Well you were speaking about men and erections."

"Yea and where would you be going with this Brian?"

"Well, my main reason for being angry is those men you be with on TV. You can't tell me you don't feel erections from them."

"So we're back to my infidelities on a fucking TV show. This is what I mean, you are so fucking insecure. Risha stood up. I have to get out of here."

"But,"

"No, No buts, I got to go now"

"I'll help you get your things together and tomorrow,"

"TOMMORROW! HAHAHA, Risha looked up at the ceiling. Lord, he ain't listening." I was listening but I figured given enough time I could change her mind.

"No kiss goodbye."

"No kiss good-by. Don't worry you will be all right, we all will be all right." She closed the door. I stood there, wondering now what do I do?

...ON THE OTHER SIDE OF TOWN...

THINGS HAD FALLEN apart down in the abyss. Due to mismanagement, Russell's money problems had reached the critical stage. His business dissolved itself when it was found he and his workers smoked the crack like it was being grown in the back lot. The responsibility of repayment fell to Russell first then his family. Torture before death was the usual way to go in this type of situation but it was learned Russell had a rich brother and sister in law. Knowing this Damian could see that recouping his losses looked pretty good and he stood to make a profit if all went well. He informed Russell that no matter what, blood was going to spill in three days but nobody has to die if he gets triple the original amount owed plus interest due him, roughly twenty-five thousand and Russell gets to choose between himself and his family. If he missed the deadline by one second everybody dies and will never be found. The final stipulation was nothing in his name better get back to him. Russell's back was against the wall, a familiar spot he found himself in often.

"Goddamn habit always fucking up shit." Now he had to do the one thing he swore he would never do again.

It was a hell of a lot more at stake now than before that little break in with Mama. He wished he could have explained to Mama that because of him nobody was hurt in that robbery. He wanted more and could have gotten more if he had used his friends but a price might have been paid in the interim and that he was not willing to accept. He shuddered at the thought of how close he was of letting those crazy ass dope heads loose on his family members. He witnessed first hand what they were capable of the day they hit one of their own cousin's homes on the east side. Talk about a shocker. As soon as they opened the door, all five of them ran in the house in a commando style surprise attack. There were two babies about five and seven and a babysitter in the living room. Russell was under the impression nobody was home, information he received from the cousin. Everybody started screaming at once. In a sudden rush to quell the noise of the occupant's frightened cries, Freddy picked up the seven year old and threw him into the wall full force. The babysitter got a mouth full of shoe while a table lamp smashed into the side of her head opening up a deep gash. A pillow smothered the other youngster after getting punched in the face. It became an every man for himself situation as they ransacked the house and then torched it. They were all so high with the exception of Russell that comprehending the scope of what was being done escaped them. Russell knew better than to have his fingerprints on anything other than what he stole. His whole objective was to get as far away as possible from his associates as he now referred them as. The group split up the minute they all were outside the house without so much as a goodbye. Russell hung back and carried the babysitter and the two youngsters a safe distance outside of the burning house. The babysitter's young body felt good in his arms. It had been a while and being so close brought back a flood of good memories. Russell slid his hands over her breasts allowing the beginnings of a stirring to build up inside his loins. He stopped and looked around. Another time he thought so he picked up his share of the stolen property and jogged off. The news was already out about what went down before any of five house robbers were off the property good.

Early that next morning Mr. Rosenthal who kept his ears open for the slightest whisper of some type of financial gain benefitting him welcomed his first customer, Starman. He received that name from always looking up to the sky in a semi coma state, a side effect from dusting out years ago. He slept in the alley around the corner next to the garbage cans waiting for the pawnshop to open. He plunked down different types of jewelry on the counter while looking around with that air of guilt all of his customers seemed to have.

"Good Morning Star boy, Mr. Rosenthal beamed, what can I do for you?"

"That's Starman fool. How much for the jewelry?" Mr. Rosenthal rarely took out his instruments for these crooks because no matter what, it was going to be a steal.

"Where'd you get it?"

"C'mon man stop playing, Starman half begged. You know where."

"Yea, I guess I do and you know there is a fee for unloading hot items."

"How fucking much old man?"

Mr. Rosenthal reached under his desk to the drawer that hid his legal thirty-eight and his seed money. He learned the hard way that the sound of the cash register drawer opening would put a dope fiend in a deadly trance like they had been hypnotized. Tommy, who was a faithful customer for about a year, came to his store high as hell one day to do business. Mr. Rosenthal opened the cash register to give him the amount they agreed to, when at the sound of the bell, Tommy's whole demeanor changed. He pulled a piece out of his waistband and demanded money and jewelry. He also had the nerve to take back what he brought and walk out of the store like nothing had happened. Mr. Rosenthal had retrieved his own gun and warned him to stop. His wish was to scare him but when Tommy whirled around gun in hand, Mr. Rosenthal thought for sure he was a dead man. He squeezed the trigger and didn't stop until all his bullets were spent. Being the ever perennial businessman he prepared the scene before dialing 911 emergency. He himself was under suspicion of receiving stolen property so after retrieving his money, less twenty dollars the amount he will claim the thief tried to take, Tommy's haul was hidden from view of nosy policemen.

"Here you go," Mr. Rosenthal replied.

"THIRTY DOLLARS?" C'mon man you robbing me.

"Ha, ha, ha, that's funny. Here's five extra for the joke." Starman snatched it and almost bumped into Freddy who was making his entrance. So focused on their needs, neither notices the other. All morning the neighborhood pawnshop was busy paying out small change for the big money items it received from thefts. Some items, lockets, rings, bracelets were more personal with initials or full names inscribed on them. Melted down, who will know, he thought. Dope fiends were his main source of income and if they kept coming to him as often as they did, he would be able to retire back in his native country sooner than expected. This business left a bad taste in his mouth and he hoped to get out of it before he had a change of heart. When the questionable items had accumulated to a certain degree, Mr. Rosenthal made a call on his throwaway cell.

"Are you hungry," he asked, without waiting for a hello.

"Yes, I am still hungry," came the monotone reply on the other end.

"Good, good, the food is piping hot so hurry on down and pick it up."

"I'll be there in a couple of hours." This conversation was repeated over and over again with ever changing coded messages, which kept him one, sometimes two steps in front of the police. One thing stood out though, he had this intense hatred for law enforcement of any kind. Because of this, which he couldn't help but show on many occasions in his younger days, many of the residents likened him to a kindred spirit. The frustrated police threatened him often and swore when they catch him he would certainly do time. He always smiled and said he ran an honorable business. Mr. Rosenthal became so trusted in the neighborhood that any and everybody was fair game to be victimized except him. There was an unspoken agreement to not touch him or his place of business. He'd had his close calls but retaliation for breaking the rules was swift in this hood and offenders usually paid with their life.

It took the Police two days before Starman and Freddy were picked up along with the one woman in the group. The fourth guy was found shot in the head and stuffed in a garbage can. The only things recovered from him were the clothes on his back. Two days later Russell was picked up, too high to run. All four got tried separately with Russell's case coming up last almost a year later. He heard the other three received twenty plus years because of the viciousness of the break in. The babysitter and one of the kids were doing fine by now but the babysitter was so traumatized she didn't remember anything usable to the case. The other kid who was slammed against the wall was still in bad shape. His extensive brain injuries meant a bleak future for this one. Russell got time served for possession of stolen goods since he couldn't be placed at the scene. He left the jail feeling like a new man with a new beginning. He kicked his habit the hard way and picked up a couple of pounds to boot. Things were going to be done differently from now on. Two days later Russell could be found in a deep nod back in the abyss.

Russell spent hours trying to figure out how to score a substantial amount of money out of his brother in three day's time. Since Brian is now rich he shouldn't mind too much about getting robbed, he thought. For people like him it's only a slight inconvenience and besides insurance would cover him. Then again, where he lives is not really a good prospect since the whole damn area had cameras, and security patrols, alarms you name it. Then he would need a truck and people to help carry shit that needed to be fenced on the spot. He had to think of something easier because there were too many ways of getting caught and besides it was hard work stealing furniture. What could he do where no one gets hurt and he get his money? His face lit up. Only one thing left and it was foolproof. Kidnap the wife, get the money, and then return her unharmed to him. Russell rubbed his hands together in acknowledgement of a brilliant plan. Only thing, he was going to need a little help with this one. Russell went to see an old friend and onetime lover.

...MINK...

THERE WAS A time when Mink, formerly known by her real name Laura Jones had visions of being the next civil rights leader. The repeat stories of injustices directed at people of color weighed on her mind during a period when there were no real prominent civil rights leaders in her hometown. In college as president of the student body she became their spokesperson on a variety of issues racism included that helped change school policies. At graduation she was voted most likely to change the world. The opportunity was staring her in the face as a born leader looking to take the first step toward martyrdom. Fast forward two months, the day of her first march against a white officer who claimed self-defense in the murder of an unarmed black youth. Wanting to put her name on the radar as an up and coming spokesperson for minorities, she chose this particularly volatile case to get her feet wet. About one hundred residents had gathered to follow the young woman who brimmed with the confidence followers were searching for in their leader. Laura felt one hundred times larger than life, giving orders, listening with the concerned look of a leader to complaints and necessary actions going forward after this march was in the history books. Nine AM, the marchers, all wearing pictured t-shirts of the fallen youth locked arms, as Laura out front, bullhorn in hand got ready to take their illegal three mile march to the police station where the officer worked. It was to end there in a noisy rally demanding the officer be indicted on murder charges. At nine-ten an army of police showed with orders the small group disband immediately.

"Hold your ground my people and we will get through this together. Do not let them intimidate us into quitting." The confrontation was expected, it was needed to slingshot Laura into the big leagues as a major player of civil rights. Her phone calls prior to the march brought the one lone reporter from some obscure channel to cover the day's events which after a quick interview, he was promised of finishing it at the end of the march. Despite the warnings they moved forward in the name of those fallen soldiers of past causes. Laura's huge ego mixed with being young and inexperienced was her recipe for disaster. She did not take it upon herself to interview the family for whom she was marching for. It usually takes only one to alter the course of events and in this case it was two brothers of the deceased that seized this opportunity to strike back at those who they felt were the cause of their family's extreme anguish. Rocks and bottles flew from the two who were hidden inside the crowd necessitating a counterattack none of the marchers were prepared for. Gripped by outright fear, mass hysteria ensued as the violent clash claimed nameless victims from age five to sixty-five, excluding their leader who revealed in the moment of truth she was not the brave person they thought she was. The bullhorn lay at the spot it was dropped as its owner ran screaming through the street knocking aside anyone in her way. Many marchers were locked up or sent to the hospital but Laura managed to escape without a scratch. Wearing her shame like a blanket, she bought a one-way ticket out of town as police and pissed off residents alike looked for her. Laura was petrified of being found out and held up to public ridicule so when she boarded the plane everything in her life that even remotely resembled Laura stayed there. It's pretty devastating to find out you are a coward in such a public way. This would be a secret Laura who changed her name to Mink will go to the grave with.

She got off broke and alone and at the lowest point in her young life with no hint of what to do next. Lucky for her, Damian happened to be at the airport that day. He introduced himself and as they say the rest is history.

"Good to know you still with the living."

"Russell. When did the devil allow you to come out and play? Whatever you need, I AIN'T GOT IT," she began closing the door.

"Seventy-five thousand dollars," Mink's head reappeared.

"This better not be no bullshit, she huffed. Hurry up and come in." When she looked to see if any other ears were in the vicinity, Russell smacked her on the behind as he walked past.

"So how's tricks."

"Touch this ass again without money in your hand and you will get shot. State your business quick before my man comes home." One look told Russell Mink was a former shell of what she used to be. When he last saw her Damian had kicked her out after beating the hell out of her.

"You know girl, you still looking good," Russell said with a devilish grin on his face.

"Sorry I can't say the same for you."

"You know, Russell ignored her remark, I think a freebie is called for just for me bringing you along in my plans." Mink knew what he was referring to when he first came out with that looking good girl shit. Russell, at this stage in the game did not have any scruples about whom he fucked and neither did Mink, but freebie?

"Tell me the plan first."

Russell grinned dropping his pants to the floor.

"This first." His scarred gnarly legs showed the true depth of his addiction. The long line of needle tracks from long ago dried up veins still marked the areas where blood had once traveled freely. His small shriveled up penis showed no signs of expanding to its full length of six point five inches. In fact he couldn't remember the last time he had an erection but today was different. He was on top of the world for the moment and the feeling below was a testament to that.

"Okay, but I'm warning you, you better not be bullshitting about that money. I'll give you five minutes."

"That's more than enough time pretty lady." Mink touched the little piece of meat with revulsion.

"When was the last time you washed?"

"Aw c'mon, I know you've had worse." It was true, the loss of respect for yourself coupled with a need to survive compels a woman to do distasteful things. It wasn't hard to see there were other forces at work here with Russell's appearance though. It's been a long journey from that day in the airport when what she thought was a little bit of good luck in meeting Damian actually was the opposite. She was still luckier than all the other girls he picked up at the airport weekly. His problem with her is that she could not be broken completely. He beat, starved and forced her to become addicted and still she would not do his bidding. She was too intelligent for her own good and a little too old. Damian got tired of wasting his time so she was put out to fend for herself. Once again she had nowhere to go but now she also had a monkey on her back. Her descent was rapid, the pull of the damned dragging her down into a dark hole where escape was impossible for those who had given up on life. Mink decided this money Russell spoke of would be her redemption.

Yea, Russell wasn't that bad at all considering what he had to offer. She closed her eyes and took all of him into her mouth.

A Minute Later

"OH MY GOD! Russell crowed. DAMN, you are the best. He carried on like there was no tomorrow. Strangely, his reaction fascinated Mink so, she tried that much harder to give the man some kind of pleasure. His penis never did get hard, but for Russell it was still the best blowjob ever.

...SIMPLE PLAN...

R USSELL AND MINK staked out the estate for two days waiting for the right opportunity. If Russell was aware of having one day left on Damian's threat, he didn't act like it. Most of his time in the car was spent being still and enjoying a comfortable high which he couldn't get enough of. The only downside was mink's incessant chatter about being bored or hot. As the heroin kicked in, as usual all movements slowed down to a lethargic snails pace as his head shook in appreciation for another good high achieved while lapsing into a deep nod. Mink stared at him in disgust only because she knew they both were slaves to a chemical that controlled their every thought, a force so strong it pushed them to do demonic deeds in order to undergo a temporary out of mind experience that was slowly eroding all traces of their essence. Mink could not restrain herself from lighting up a rock as long as she was around Russell. It was her pledge that after she got her money the habit would be the first thing to deal with on her way back up. It was another cruel acknowledgement of a past she needed to let go.

"I thought you stopped smoking that shit?" Russell murmured.

"Leave me alone," Mink said exhaling as she spoke. As luck would have it Risha's limo passed, heading south toward Mother Allerton's. Mink started the engine of the stolen Mazda and followed from about three blocks away.

Risha was torn. She wasn't sure if this was the right thing to do but something had to be done. She decided to call later to make sure Brian was all right, but at the moment a drink was in order. Wrong, a lot of drinks will be needed for this one. She had Dale drop her by Moody's, which was her favorite bar for well-known people who want to be unknown. Risha stepped out and told him he might as well leave, she was going to be there awhile.

"You sure Mrs. Marshall, I don't mind waiting."

"No, go home to your family and tell Linda hi. I'll catch a cab when I'm ready."

It was early in the evening and the real hard drinkers hadn't come in from their twelve-hour manual labor jobs yet. The crowd that gathered here most evenings was construction workers from the surrounding area. At around six the place is transformed into a living, breathing horde of beer guzzling workers letting off steam from another day in the trenches. Risha could barely understand a word that was spoken and that was okay, she hadn't come to socialize, just people watch and drink. The 72" flat screen T.V. boasted sports channels showing their countrymen playing their form of football. Most times she would sit for a few hours allowing her brain to shift into stand-by mode for a while.

"Hard day, Ms. Allerton?"

"Yea, pretty fucked up you could say. Keep em' coming Carl." Risha picked a secluded corner to begin her cascade into numbing oblivion. She thought about her marriage and the last argument they had which in reality was a one sided blow up on her part. By her third drink she came to a sober conclusion. She was the problem all along.

Mink parked the car across the street and turned it off.

"What do we do now genius, go in and drag her ass out of there?"

"Nah, relax, we wait a little bit, let her get a few drinks down so it'll be easier to control her and get out of here with no trouble.

"When you get so smart, that's a good idea."

"Yea, I always think good when I'm high. The better the shit, the better I think."

Risha was on her eighth maybe tenth drink and drunk. Her husbands face had invaded her mind and stayed there. She searched so hard to find this man and yet she was the one who wasn't ready. Everything about Brian, she loved. He was in her through and through where she wanted him to be and being drunk could not erase that fact. What he had become, she created out of her own misguided self-absorbed attitude. This is the only man that's ever loved her despite what she put him through. She didn't see that then but now it was clear. It is settled, there will be big changes once she got back home. Risha stood up,

"A CELEBRATION. I'M STILL A HAPPILY MARRIED WOMAN. ANOTHER DRINK CARL AND TRY TO MAKE THEM A LITTLE STRONGER. Risha fumbled around for her phone.

-BRIAN, I LOVE YOU. Come get me, I was foolish…"

"RISHA, RISHAA, WHAT DID YOU SAY, WHERE ARE YOU?" I could hear Risha talking to the bartender about her drinks but she had taken her ear from the phone. My heart was beating so hard it hurt from the surprise phone call. There were so many things I needed to tell her. This was my wake up call, loud and clear. There was no way in hell I was going to let my sweet wife down again.

Risha's phone slipped out of her hand and in her inebriated state she managed to step on it in her haste to pick it up. Silence, of all times for the call to drop, I thought. The joy I had soured with every unanswered press of the redial button until my calls went straight to voicemail. Frantic, my mind sifted through bars she could be at and friends to call. My first thought was the bar where we first met for drinks but knowing her she would be somewhere more private. I called there anyway with the expected results. Her colleague came to mind but that was a lesson already learned. He wouldn't have any idea.

"I can't serve you any more liquor Mrs. Allerton, you've reached your limit."

"What the hell you mean I reached my limit. On second thought, you're right Carl, please point me to the door."

"Would you like me to call your driver?"

"Called already, ugh, urp, arghhh, a waterfall of vomit coated the floor to the dismay of the bartender. SOMEBODY CLEAN THAT UP," Risha indicated. By the time Mink stepped up to the door of the bar, Risha wobbled her way out. Mink grabbed hold of her and helped her to the car. Thirty minutes passed and not a word from Risha. I paced the floor until the thought of Dale hit me.

"He would know where she's at," I shouted to no one. The bedroom is turned upside down, every place paper is stored is searched and I'm upset again. The only number is in her phone. I have phone nos. and addresses of every man considered to be a threat to my marriage and nothing on the driver who I trusted to ensure Risha's safety every day. The show's office got a call but all I got was an answering machine. I'm right back at square one, waiting.

"Damn, you fast. Risha pushed away as she stepped back to take a good look at Mink.

-Who the hell is you?" She said, wavering from side to side as she did.

"I'm your driver."

"Brian sent you for me?"

"Yea, whatever," Mink answered. Risha plopped down in the seat next to Russell.

"Honey you came for me," She opened her arms and passed out. As mink pulled away from the curb, Risha's eyes popped open.

"Slow this car down before I puke. Her head, the car or the world was spinning around like the blades on a fan on a hot summer day, she didn't know which. GODDAMN, I feel sick," she said before she passed out again.

After they arrived in mink's apartment, Russell got ready to put the second half of his plan into action. He couldn't believe how hard this was becoming. A bad feeling washed over him as soon as Risha was in the car and worsened when they got into the house. This is not a stranger in the street, this is family. The woman he held hostage in the next room had, behind his brother's back, come down to the Abyss more than once to help him out with money, food, clothes and medicine. All his associates looked forward to her visits. It was too late to turn back now but more important it was a fix for the greater of two evils. This had to be done no matter how distasteful the feeling. Russell masked his voice as he made the call from a prepaid cell.

"Risha?"

"Brian Marshall?" I looked at my caller ID. I didn't recognize the number but he got the name right.

"Yea, who is this?"

"I'm your wife's kidnapper and we have to get some things straight about how we gonna handle this small problem."

"Who's wife, is this some kind of a fucking joke? I just talked to my wife about an hour ago."

"No joke, Mr. Marshall. Your wife's name is Risha Allerton, right." A flash of my life tied into Risha's shot through my mind in that one instant giving me the feeling I had just died. The only word to escape me was yes before the caller spoke again.

"She's going to be okay as long as you do exactly what I tell you. Look at your watch. From Two am until noon we will need you to put together seventy-five thousand dollars. Any police, she's dead. Tell anyone, she's dead. We'll be watching so do the right thing by your wife and she will be back with you before you know it. The phone went dead and I sat there stunned for the second time in twenty-four hours. I knew somehow it was my fault that Risha fell into the hands of kidnappers and lord knows what else. I had to do something but what? It was now two fifteen. She was in their hands for the rest of the night and half the next day. Making the right decision was imperative for Risha to be back in my arms again. With police the chances of them blowing the whole undercover thing are always good. Half the time they won't believe a word you say until something happens, so they will be left out of the picture for now.

Things were going according to the plan so far. The thought of too good to be true crossed Russell's mind knowing Brian as he did. His brother might not go along with the plans as he laid them out and this was much too important to get fucked up. He went into the bedroom where the two women were.

"I'm going to make sure things are taken care of so there won't be any mess ups. You think you'll be okay by yourself with Risha?"

"I'll be fine, just you go get my money."

"You know you can keep the door closed and watch TV, she's tied up pretty good."

"You afraid I'm going to hurt your little movie star."

"Yea, as a matter of fact I am. You seemed a little angry at her on our way here."

"Why would I be angry at her, I don't know the woman, Mink said in her best innocent sounding voice. She'll be fine."

"Okay, I'll be back as soon as possible."

"Yea, yea, bring me back some shit when you come in." The door couldn't close fast enough.

"WAKE UP! MO-nique'." It took Risha a few seconds to open heavy eyelids and then only part way. Her body hurt but the putrid odor of fresh vomit on her clothes caused a wave of dry heaves until a dribble of bile dropped down to blend in with the rest of the puke. She was aware of restraints binding her involuntary movements and now gave that her full attention. A few firm yanks answered the small question leading to a much bigger one as fear threatened to overcome her need to be calm and focused. Talk and find out what they want, Risha. Give Brian enough time to find and save you like he promised. This has to be about money, nothing more. Stay calm, deep breaths, she repeated while her heart tried to punch a hole through her chest cavity. In the dark room, her eyes rested on the figure of a crazed looking woman staring down at her. Mink stood there slapping a belt on her palm her mind set on revenge. Risha knew at once seeing the look in Mink's eyes that it was Monique' she was looking at.

"OH boy, I'm in a lot of trouble, right?"

"No more than your usual, Mo-nique'." Risha had to start thinking. Being kidnapped because of a character is something she never expected.

"Miss, My real name is Risha. Monique' is a person I pretend to be."

"All of us are pretending to be somebody else but what you did don't make it right"

"If you saw something you didn't like, I apologize. All lines are read from a script for the show, nothing more. Please, I mean you no harm, can you please let me go."

"You finished? You know I could'a been famous too. I was smart and people used to look up to me. All I wanted was my chance at making it big but one little mistake was all it took for me to be condemned for life and it wasn't even my fault. Them two fucking boys should'a been killed for what they done to me but here I am with your trifling ass. You make it big and now you think you better than everybody. I deserve to be rich and famous and mean to people. Why can't I have my turn.

"I know you're hurting from what those boys did to you and believe me whatever it was I'm sorry you had to go through such a traumatic time in your life. But if you let me go, I promise I'll get you a part in my show so you can become rich and famous."

"Shut up, you lie and use people all the time, probably lying to me right now. Don't think I don't know how your slick ass operates." Mink let go with a stinging strike across Risha's face with her belt. She then sat down in a chair where her pipe lay on the table and lit up. Her crossed right leg swung nervously as she blew the smoke in Risha's direction. Jumping up, she walked to Risha, turned and sat back down. She seemed unsure of what to do. The sting of that belt and the rising welt on Risha's face was a glimpse of worse to come and she sensed it. Staying alive was all that mattered so she could put this crackhead bitch behind bars. What scared her more was the fact she couldn't have done this alone. Where were her friends? Mink answered that question for her.

"Where the hell is Russell with our money," She peeked out the window to the left and then to the right. RUSSELL? Is she talking about my brother in-law, Risha wondered. She had never seen this woman before on her visits to help Russell and her, she would have remembered. Mink started talking again about her character on the show. Risha was so busy trying to figure out her next move she ignored Mink until Mink got right in her face.

"I ASKED YOU A QUESTION BITCH. WHEN I ASK YOU A QUESTION, YOU ANSWER IT." Mink raised the belt high and sent it whistling through the air striking Risha on her ear. Her body contorted from the unexpected swipe but before she could cry out another swish and another until Risha begged her to stop. Too far gone to stop, Mink began using her fists, her flailing punches missing more than they hit. When she did connect a cut was opened over Risha's right eye while another errant blow caught her in the lip.

"PLEASE, PLEASE, WHAT WAS YOUR QUESTION?" Mink stopped and tried to think.

"Fuck, I don't remember. You should'a answered it the first time. She backhanded Risha with a closed fist uprooting a tooth. Mink squealed shaking her hand.

"You did that on purpose." Risha remained quiet, fearful that the slightest move might provoke more lunacy. She knew this strange woman had no boundaries she would not cross and the thought of death became a real possibility. Mink looked at the open wound on the back of her hand, then disappeared into the bathroom giving Risha an opportunity to try and free herself. Her thoughts went to the accomplices she hadn't seen yet. Lord knows if they are men and she was sure they were and anything like Mink she was in for a brutal time. It was imperative to get out at all costs. Mink emerged from the bathroom, picked up her pipe and went to the kitchen. Risha went back to where she left off.

"Oh Mo-niiique', I have something for you. Risha heard her coming in from the kitchen. Her fingers moved faster at the sound of Mink's threatening voice. She couldn't stop, she was close, almost there. Mink came up behind her and wrapped one arm around her neck pulling her up. Risha couldn't see the six-inch kitchen knife that was plunged deep into her chest. She opened her mouth to a silent scream as her terror filled eyes slowly lost their luster with every beat of her damaged heart until they were void of life. Mink had pulled a chair up in front of the woman so she could have a front row seat to see what dying looked like. After it was said and done, Mink closed Risha's eyes and shrugged.

"There, now you have a nice sleep Monique." She went into the living room and turned on the TV.

The bus driver sat not paying Russell any mind who was standing at the curb for twenty minutes watching him and wishing there was something he could do to him. At a specified time the bus rumbled the ten feet it took to get to the legal stop and opened its doors. At two thirty in the morning it was a blessing to at least have a bus there at the curb even if he wasn't ready for passengers yet. Mink's apartment was one block from the last stop in the ghetto, which was still better than Russell's place which included a ten block walk for the bus. The ride would be two hours because of a transfer and the fact his brother lived uptown with the white folks. I'll be calling a taxi when I leave outta there Russell thought still fuming that it took so long. One ring of the doorbell brought me running until I saw who it was.

Russell I don't have time for you now, what are you doing here this time of morning anyway.

"Is everything all right? I heard Risha got taken on account of a bad debt I owe and from the look on your face it's true."

"You mean to tell me because of your debt, my Risha is in trouble."

"Look man, I didn't know these fools would stoop so low to get their money."

"How the hell they know we were brothers."

"Man, I bragged to everyone my brother was married to Risha, Fucking, Allerton."

"Now is not the time to get all excited."

"I'm sorry, I didn't mean nothing by it. I'm here to help, if I can. This is some fucked up shit those creeps did."

"What are you talking about, YOU WOULD DO THE SAME KIND OF SHIT, probably have already. All you dope fiend motherfuckers would do damn near anything for a dollar." Russell took offense to my accusation.

"Yea Lil bro, I've done my share of dirt but some things even I won't do. I wish you had lent me the money and maybe this shit would not have gone down."

"My money doesn't have anything to do with you and your fucked up life. Anyway it ain't about you right now. I got to figure out what to do and quick."

"Well, I don't think she's in any real kind of danger."

"And how the hell would you know that Russell." My anger towards him was growing by the second.

"The kind of people I know just want their money back and they'll go to certain extremes to show they mean business but murder is a whole 'nother level which I've never seen them go to.

"So you mean torture or god forbid rape which is still torture is what they'd do instead."

"Nah, They just trying to send me a message through you that's all."

"Sounds like you know them quite well. How about names and addresses."

"Come on, you know they don't work like that. The only guy I know is Crater and he's like me, a nobody. He's their runner and like go between. I did run a couple of jobs for them though, you know to put a little change in my pocket so I seen how they operate. If they get paid, you should be all right."

"I need Risha to be all right. It was my fault in the first place she's in this mess. Because of my jealousy, she wound up in a bar drinking by herself trying to figure out what to do about me. She calls me and says she'll give me one more chance and to come get her. Can you believe that, I get a second chance and she gets kidnapped. What are the fucking odds? I was hoping she would see all the missed calls and messages from me. I don't know, maybe she couldn't by that time. I need to do more, Risha's counting on me. I think I'm going to call the police."

"Hold up Brother, the police, are you sure?"

"No I'm not sure. All I know is I'm going crazy sitting here waiting for morning when I need to be out looking. I need to find Dale. What do you think I should do?"

Feelings of sorrow stirred in Russell. Again he felt guilty for what he was doing and now he was up close and personal. He forced himself to think only of the money, and the fact Risha wasn't in the hands of anybody except him. Family pictures dotted the walls of many shared good times together and Russell spotted one of he and Brian at the wedding. In a rare moment of lucidity, Russell decided he needed to put right what he messed up. I must be out of my mind to do this to my little brother, he thought. Fuck it, I'll figure out another way to take care of Damian. Russell's other way was to get close enough to his problem and kill him at all costs.

"Don't worry Brian, I'll get to the bottom of this and I promise to bring Risha back to you."

"How are you going to do that," I asked with questionable faith.

"I know some people. Give me a few hours." Russell hurried back to Mink's place to get Risha. The question now was how to explain this to Mink. Hell, nothings changed except the money and she don't need to know about that until Risha's back with Brian. When Russell got there all was quiet except for the T.V. Mink was sleep on the couch.

"Mink, Russell nudged the woman until she started moving on her own. How's Risha doing?"

"Monique? That bitch is fine. Had to put her ass to sleep though, She started yelling all over the place, trying to wake the fucking dead."

"Stop fucking calling her Monique, Her name is Risha.

-Mink, You didn't do nothing stupid?"

"No, I didn't do nothing, did you get the money?"

"Not yet, I got to go and make the exchange. Russell plopped down, weak from such a long exhausting day. He needed a fix. Rubbing his eyes he pointed towards the bedroom. I got to take Risha with me, go get her." Mink went into the bedroom and came back minus Risha.

"I can't wake the bitch up."

"What do you mean you can't wake her up?" He ran into the bedroom. Risha was slumped over being held from falling by her binds. Blood had oozed out a path from her heart to the black jellied pool surrounding the chair legs. Russell gave her mouth to mouth not knowing what else to do but gave up in a quick minute. He had no air to give but it was obvious she wasn't coming back.

"MINK, WHAT THE FUCK HAPPENED! YOU FUCKING KILLED HER."

"I didn't mean to, she wouldn't stop screaming."

"WOULDN'T STOP SCREAMING? YOU COULDN'T JUST STICK A SOCK IN HER MOUTH."

"I didn't think of that at the moment."

"You smoking that damn crack shit, got your brain all fucked up."

"Fuck you!" The mention of crack prompted Mink to light up her last vial. Russell slapped it out her hand across the room. Mink shrieked as she dove on the floor after it. He sat with his head in his hands, lamenting about this new problem.

"What the hell am I gonna do now, Nobody is gonna believe me if I tell them this crazy bitch killed my sister-in-law and not me. It don't matter, either way it's jail or my family and I can't have neither one of them. There's got to be a way out of this. Russell looked at Mink sitting on the floor lighting up like nothing happened. We got to frame my brother and you gonna help me." Mink exhaled a cloud of smoke.

"I ain't doing nothing until I get my money."

"You fucked everything up so before your ass gets a dime we going to do this." Mink sucked her teeth.

"Shit, always a fucking catch."

"Bitch, come the fuck on."

One Hour Later

RUSSELL REAPPEARED AT my door followed by a female he introduced as Mink. His disposition gave the impression of good news but I wondered why bring a fellow fiend to my house.

"Fuck, this is a nice house." Mink fluttered flirtatious eyes at me. Really, Does she have any idea what's going on here?

"Russell, It's ten AM, so what's the story?"

"Mink found her. She made a few calls and sure as shit we talked to her. Did you get the money?"

"Yea, you know I wasn't going to take any chance with that. I got the seventy-five grand. So you talked to her, is she all right."

Yea she's okay, can't wait to be back in your arms. They gonna call me in an hour and a car is going to pull up with her inside. I give them the money, Risha comes home, it's all good baby brother. At the sound of that it felt like the boa constrictor that was hell bent on squeezing the life out of me had disappeared. My stomach was still in knots but I would live with that until I had her back. I wasn't keen on them knowing where we lived but after Risha is back in my arms, thanks to security cameras all over the place that problem will be handled.

"That's the best news I've heard in two days. Well then I guess we wait. And to you Mink, I thank you in advance and my wife really thanks you. Russell, when this is over you and me need to talk. I can't be having this kind of shit happening to my family. Suppose if there were kids involved, I don't even want to think about that scenario."

"Yeah, I feel you little brother, I'm gonna take care of my end so this shit don't happen no more. By the way, you have anything to drink up in this big ass house like Tequila?"

"Yea I think so, Mink would you like something." Russell gave her a look.

"Yes please, brandy for a toast."

"Toast?"

"Well yea, it'll be too much excitement in an hour so I wanted to toast now to her safe return and hopefully you catching the guys who did this."

"Don't worry about those guys, first chance I get, they are dead, but yea, I'll toast to that." I prepared myself a drink and joined my brother and friend for a quick toast. I needed something to settle my stomach down anyway.

"Brian, you got a lemon?" Russell asked.

"Lemon chaser? Since when you became so pretentious," I said under my breath. Any other time it would be the cheapest shit in the store and damn a chaser. Well, when in Rome I guess. Mink removed three small pills she had hidden and plopped them in the unattended drink. After a quick stir with her finger there was no hint of the tiny white substance except for the knowing smile on Russell's face.

"What's that other pill," he asked in a hushed whisper.

"It's for a guaranteed performance," she said. Russell leaned back in the chair.

"Here you go Russell, I said as I walked out of the kitchen. Okay, bottoms up!" We clinked our drinks while Mink spoke once again of Risha's safe return. I swallowed mine in one gulp, anxious to let the strong drink sooth my stomach muscles and lessen my nervousness a bit. Russell and Mink made small talk while I sat silent, my mind wandering all over the place. I thought of Risha and what I was going to do to her captors when she returned. My nerves must have been getting the best of me because my stomach was churning more than usual. I felt dizzy as I made my way to the bathroom to pop an antacid while cursing my lack of tolerance for liquor when I needed it most. Collapsing into my bed, I called out for Russell to come upstairs. He was going to have to hold it down until I felt a little better and that I was counting on him. That was all I could get out before my mind shut down.

"Brian, Brian, Where'd you put the money." Mink found her way upstairs to where we were.

"YAYY, he's knocked out, did he tell you where the money was?"

"Nah, but we got other business to take care of first. Russell looked down at his brother with a frown. You sure he's not in too deep?"

"I know what I'm doing. He's not in a coma, just dreamland. He'll cooperate once Ms. Mink get started working on him."

"Well Ms. Mink, hurry up and take off his clothes," Russell mimicked. Mink gave him the finger but did as she was told, taking great joy in seeing what she would be working with.

"DAMN RUSSELL, are you a half brother?"

"No, why would you ask a stupid question like that?"

"Look at the size of this thing, Mink stared wide eyed with obvious sexual intrigue. Wouldn't you ask?"

"Fuck you woman, just do your job."

"With pleasure," Mink answered out of earshot of Russell. She knew a nerve was touched but so what, it is what it is. This is going to be like fucking good brother, bad brother, she thought. The bad brother's only attraction is he's bad. His good looks are no more, his dick is as useless as he is as a man, and that drug problem can only make things worse. His future is an O.D. or jail and it's anybody's call which would come first. On the other hand, good brother is rich, handsome, hard working, in great shape and best of all has a big dick, which she was going to enjoy test-driving.

Russell was sitting in the corner of the room busy fumbling with a small video camera. His obvious ineptness was confirmed along with a string of curses as he lost patience but kept trying. With success at getting it to function at last, he still felt it necessary to complain to Mink about stealing shit that was hard to figure out.

"Stop fucking around and get started, he said. Mink ignored him and got to work acquiring an erection as I lay there in a drug induced state. As per Russell, she bounced up and down and made a lot of moaning sounds as he panned around trying to catch every angle. Kiss him," he ordered as the camera zoomed in close of her tongue going in my mouth. Satisfied with what they had, he ordered Mink to help get Risha out the car reminding her to first add some scratches and bruises. Alone now, she thrust without the irritating direction from Russell stopping the action every time she started to get aroused. It wouldn't take long to finish what had been started with a few more well placed thrusts. In heeding to Russell's wishes, her nails raked Brian's backside as obscenities of delight were screamed out in hushed tones. She bit down into his neck, trembling as she came to her own fitting conclusion, only then collapsing out of breath on top of an inert body.

"Baby you are the best live dildo I ever fucked and the only. I can only imagine what you could do for me if you was awake." She shook her head and went to join Russell in the garage.

"It's about time, help me drag this bitch upstairs."

"Hell no, the bitch is staring at me. I ain't fucking with her."

"Shit you killed her, you lucky she don't come back and whip your ass. Stick to the plan or we going to prison."

"Okay, Okay, why we taking her upstairs anyway?"

"You know what, you got a point. Let's put her in the trunk of Brian's car."

"You got the money?"

"What the hell you think I was doing while you upstairs fucking?"

"Handling your business like I handled mine." Mink answered with the smile of a satisfied woman.

...QUESTIONS AND ANSWERS...

A FEW PHONE CALLS brought the world at the doorstep of Five Pearlmon Lane. They had arrived an hour ago making sure to keep the quiet until all their I's were dotted and T's crossed. It was important to leave nothing to chance one-way or the other. An anonymous call could be a nut stirring up some trouble or a neighbor that saw something out of the ordinary. One detail that raised an eyebrow was the fact, Mrs. Allerton missed two days on the set and did not call for any reason. Not her style and it was also known about all the crazy ass stalker Monique haters she'd reported time and again. The driver too was worried about not being able to reach her after he'd gone to the residence to pick her up with no response even though the car was in the garage and the TV was on. The residence was surrounded and a search warrant was a phone call away. A voice on a bullhorn sounded asking me to open the door. I was at once awake with Risha on my mind. Calling out her name I damn near had to pinch myself to make sure this wasn't a dream. The sudden commotion was confusing with simultaneous sounds of the bullhorn again along with my cell phone and the doorbell exploding into the quiet and invading my groggy head. Barely able to gather my thoughts, I wondered what the hell was going on as I grabbed a robe taking notice of my nakedness. Lots of things crossed my mind as I ran down the stairs to open the door for a bunch of impatient people. I felt sore all over but more important the money was not where I put it, which could be good or bad news. No Russell and no money then Risha should be here unless something went very wrong. I heard voices as I approached the door.

"It's the police, Mr. Marshall, please open the door."

"Police? Oh my God, please tell me you have my wife."

"That's what we need to talk to you about, sir." Behind them a multitude of camera flashes popped left and right similar to the twinkling of stars in the sky. Before I knew what was happening an invasion of twenty or so officers in blue rushed in to form a border encompassing me. A detective sat me down and started with questions without bothering to explain why my rights were being violated. They stood there unmoving with hands behind their backs like perfect little soldiers waiting on orders to do God only knows what. Before answering his questions, I needed to know what was half the world doing at my house?

"Calm down Mr. Marshall, this will be over in a minute. The detective put his hand on my shoulder in a friendly gesture as he talked. You know my wife is a big fan of your wife, never misses an episode. Now, could you please tell us where she is?"

"Last thing I remember she was with the kidnappers?"

"Kidnappers? That's a new one. We know nothing of a kidnap. Are you sure about this? It couldn't be something else." His partner walked over talking to someone on the phone while we spoke.

"Yes I'm sure. The kidnappers called me, I believe yesterday and warned me not to speak to anyone, especially you. I was trying to handle her release on my own but I got sick and passed out."

"So the story you're going with is she was kidnapped. His partner's hand went up signaling the search warrant was signed and the line of police moved into different locations of the house.

"That's not a story, who called you? My head followed all the back and forth action that was taking place around me. Destruction also could be heard going on in different parts of the estate. Look, I don't know how you found out about what's going on here but now that you know I think it is imperative you act quickly on my wife's behalf. Make some calls and find out where she is and if she's okay."

"Don't worry Mr. Marshall we'll get down to the bottom of this. So you say you can't recall what day she was, as you say kidnapped. Why is that? I know I for one would remember the exact moment my wife was kidnapped."

"I know what day she was kidnapped, I don't know what day it is now. I told you I passed out and I don't know how long.

"Hmm, interesting or did your mind deliberately blank out the events of the pass few days concerning all things with your wife."

"That's not true and I would appreciate it if you did not alter what I say to you."

"Okay Mr. Marshall, you were sleep. Do you take drugs?"

"No!"

"Will you give us permission to administer drug test on you?"

"Of course, I have nothing to hide. The detective paused a moment to go over his notes. So you say phone calls have to be made. Are there others involved in this so called kidnapping and what would be their names?"

"I don't know how many. Look, I was just following orders so I could get my wife back home. They demanded a seventy-five thousand dollar ransom and if I complied which I did she'd be returned unharmed."

"Did you and your wife have a good relationship?"

"Do you and your wife have a good relationship?"

"As a matter of fact no, but my wife is still a phone call away. So I ask you to please stop taking my questioning as a personal attack on your character. I don't know you and I sure as hell don't know if you're lying about her kidnapping or if she's missing for whatever reason. Do we have an understanding? I acquiesced. Good, answer the question please."

"We had an up and down marriage. She walked out on me the same day she was kidnapped." That didn't sound right to my ears but I continued on. I got a call from her later from a bar asking me to come pick her up. She had been drinking, I guess due to our fighting and forgot to tell me where she was."

"You ever put your hands on her, Mr. Marshall."

"Hell no. I'm not that kind of man."

"Well, I couldn't help but notice that there's some broken furniture around. Was that your doing?"

"Breaking furniture is not the same as physical violence."

"It is if she's thrown into it, Mr. Marshall." A policeman whispered something in the detective's ear. He looked at the other detective who put his booklet in his pocket. Four more officers joined us.

"Mr. Marshall, please stand up." The change in attitude was apparent as the detectives grabbed hold of each wrist. My robe popped open as I rose and I attempted to tie it more securely.

"We'll do that, please hold your hands out." An officer folded my hands behind my back and slapped a set of handcuffs on me.

"DOES ANYBODY HERE KNOW WHAT THE HELL THEY ARE DOING? I'M NOT THE ONE THAT SHOULD BE GETTING ARRESTED, I DIDN'T DO ANYTHING! WHAT YOU NEED TO BE DOING IS FINDING MY WIFE!"

"Sir, don't worry about your missing wife, we found her."

"WHAT, WHERE, CAN I SEE HER?"

"She's dead, Mr. Marshall. Murdered and stuffed in the trunk of your car. But I'm sure you already knew that." The word murdered echoed in my ears with no meaning attached to it. What did that mean, she was murdered. Who was he talking about? I tried to speak, to get a clearer meaning of the word that seemed to provoke such anger.

"Those scratches, he used his Billy club to further push aside what my robe was covering up. Bruises and more scratches, looks to me like you been in a fight Mr. Marshall." By this time the crowd outside had grown two fold with reporters rushing to the house in an attempt to be first at getting the story aired.

The same rags that covered my wedding were here to compare then and now and offer their abstract view on the events in my life. The police hustled me to a waiting cruiser stopping for a moment so the media could take humiliating snapshots of me. The noonday sun shined bright but all I saw was darkness. My world, my life as I knew it was over. My head hung low in despair, something was very wrong and it had something to do with this word, murdered. A sudden jolt of pain reverberated through my head after being bounced off of the closed door of the police cruiser before being shoved in.

"It was an accident," the guilty officer later noted with a smirk. That brought me back into reality. Risha was dead and wherever she was I needed to be there to protect her. Beating my head against the window of the squad car didn't work, so a well-placed kick at the window blew it out bringing the police running with their guns drawn. Frantically, I rubbed my neck around the edges of the broken out frame hoping for a sharp fragment to slice my neck open. A gang of policemen wrestled me out of the car and subdued me until I could be placed in another vehicle with an escort.

"You ain't getting outta this shit that easy murderer. You gonna pay for killing Mrs. Allerton for the rest of your sorry life." The cop took his right boot and stepped on my head mushing my face into the ground. They lifted me up for transfer to the van, found out I wouldn't walk so I was dragged.

Instead of waking up in a cell I found myself handcuffed to a hospital bed. It didn't matter, moving any body part proved too painful. It seemed I went berserk in the van and had to be overcome by any means, which culminated to a knockout after a very thorough beating with clubs, feet and fists. My throbbing head was battling my stomach for the title of worse pain and remembering what day it is was becoming a full time job for me. The nurse came running at the press of a button to add more medication. It seems two more days had elapsed that escaped my memory although this time there was proof of my whereabouts.

When I received an all clear, the police wasted no time in delivering me to jail like they were sticking it to me. Hell, right now where else could I go with the hospital besieged with people trying a get a view of the killer of Monique'. Yes, jail was looking pretty good right now except I had to put up with the escort, that one black police officer who is the spokesperson for all of the Black race.

"You ain't fooling anybody. I have been on the force for twenty-two years so I know a lying motherfucker when I see one. You pretend you all shook up but the reality of it is your poor ass lucked out and married a rich black woman and that wasn't good enough for you. You had to have it all and as usual punks like you make all of us look bad. I hope they electrocute your ass." And as usual fools like him don't have a clue.

When we got to the precinct, first thing the police did was throw me in a forty by fifty room with three other prisoners that were picked up sometime previously and ordered us to strip. There were two policemen and three policewomen present. A young man next to me protested their presence and received a nasty swipe to the knee by a club for his trouble.

"Are there any more complaints?" The male cop said with a smirk. Missing badges on all their uniforms meant 'not me' and 'I don't know' were the only ones in the room so being quiet and doing as they instructed was best even if it was an affront to our dignity. This for me was just added punishment I deserved for allowing Risha to be taken away from me. When they were through debasing us in every way they could think of, the head he-woman announced in as masculine a voice as possible how they were the caretakers of a system we were now residing in and it was up to us if we wanted to do easy or hard time.

I was taken into an interrogation room and handcuffed to a chair. Two hours they left me to replay the chain of events over and over in my head. What could I have done differently? Thinking now, there was nothing I did right. My biggest mistake was in letting Russell who is a lowlife handle the transaction with fellow lowlifes. I should have known better than to let fiends come to my house, which more than likely seemed like a castle in their eyes. From the moment they set foot on my property was probably when a decision was made to renege on their end of the bargain, taking much more than the seventy-five thousand cash. Risha must have been killed to protect their identity and seeing that I was out cold, I became the perfect patsy to frame as insurance the police never look in any other direction. Russell and his friend must have gotten snatched as well and they too are possibly dead by now. Things will never be the same again and since I'm still among the living I guess I'm the man for the job of killing all those involved. Whoever they are better keep checking over their shoulder because their days now have a number attached to it and the clock is ticking. Two interrogators entered and immediately started firing accusations at me. 'I don't know' was my answer to every question. After the shouting, one of them sat at the table and tried to make me come to my senses and admit to killing my wife.

"By the way, let me see here, you tested positive for gamma-hydroxybutyrate, acetylsalicylic, bismuth subsalicylate and sildenafil citrate. That sounds like you had a hell of a party to me."

"I didn't understand anything you just said but it doesn't matter, I didn't do anything."

"Well here's what I think Mr. Marshall. Let me see if I can help you put all the pieces together. He explained my every move from the moment I supposedly got high until they came knocking. After he finished a pad and pen was pushed towards me. You don't have to say anything, just write it down. I understand that it was an accident and in a moment of panic you tried to cover the crime up. Who could blame you, this is a lot of trouble you got yourself into but it's time to do the right thing." I picked up the pen, looked at him briefly and wrote, 'Lawyer.'

The interrogator frowned, balled the paper up and threw it at me. Both of them left the room leaving me to sit for another two hours before an officer came in and led me to a cell. His timing couldn't be better. I was about to give them another charge to add to my record for peeing on their floor. When you are famous and loved the judicial process will work in overdrive to convict. I wasn't in the cell a day before being called to appear in front of the judge. He asked if I had an attorney to represent me. On my non-answer he called out to a man sitting off to the side of the courtroom busy shuffling papers. The man got up and hurried to the front dropping papers as he went.

"This one's for you."

"Yes your honor." He requested a continuance for a new date before taking me to a separate meeting room. My Attorney's name was Herbert Olanawitz.

"Hello Mr. Marshall," He extended a sweaty hand for me to shake leaving the feeling of having squeezed a wet spongy ball. He dropped his five foot six-inch, two hundred-fifty plus frame down on a wooden chair made for leaner sizes. The old chair groaned under the weight but held fast. He was a rural small town boy, kept to himself and physically, a doctor's worse nightmare, but book smart, the kind of man who was voted to be your boss someday. I bet he passed the bar on his first go round and with a very high score no doubt. Foregoing the pleasantries I got right to the point.

"Could you tell me a little about yourself since you're representing me?"

"Sure Mr. Marshall." His eager response to my question was an indication of how much of a pompous ass he was already. Herbert interlocked his fat fingers on the table and looked skyward for a second. Let's see, I graduated third in my class at Harvard, my father was a lawyer who helped me to understand the system so I have a good amount of knowledge on how things work in this state. I grew up in Latte River Valley, a small town in Nebraska and attended the best private schools money could buy. I passed the bar on my first try and I will do what it takes to win this case for you. I believe in innocence until guilt is proven beyond a shadow of a doubt."

"I don't mean to cut in but how many successful cases do you have under your belt?"

"Well, you will be my first, but I assure you, I am a very competent attorney." Oh lord, I'm this fool's guinea pig. I tried to remain calm, give him a chance, maybe he is what he says.

"Okay, Okay, you at least heard a little about my case. Tell me what you think."

"Mr. Marshall, It's a little premature to discuss the case as of yet. I will be collecting data from many different sources prior to analyzing and separating the facts from fiction. Give me a week and I will get back to you. Now it's my turn to ask you a few questions and you must be completely transparent with me."

"Transparent?"

"Truthful, Mr. Marshall, No hidden secrets."

"I understood what you said, Mr. Olanawitz. I have no reason to lie."

"Sure, now you say in the report that you did not kill her. Could you explain how Mrs. Allerton was found in the trunk of your car?"

"If I knew that, wouldn't it suggest that I might have had a hand in her murder?"

"The police say they found you naked, in a dazed and drug induced state. Can you explain that?"

"They didn't find me dazed or naked. I was upset and I had on a robe which the police prevented me from re-closing prior to handcuffing me."

"I see. Remember Mr. Marshall, complete transparency."

"Look, Herbert, We haven't gotten through the first five minutes of your questions and already you're implying that I'm lying. Are you with me or against me?"

"The police say one thing and you're saying another. I'm just trying to get the facts straight between the two sides. Try not to be so defensive."

"Yea, just make sure we on the same team."

"I assure you, we are. Okay Mr. Marshall could you tell me about all that transpired leading up to the moment the police knocked on the door." I explained the whole scenario again in as much detail as possible while Mr. Olanawitz listened. At one point his cell phone rang and he talked while I talked. When I stopped, irritated that he couldn't possibly be listening to me, he looked up from his phone conversation and urged me to keep talking. After hanging up, he stood.

"You leaving?"

"Yes, I have other important matters to attend to, but when I come back we'll prepare a defense."

"You could not have possibly heard anything I said while you were on your cell."

"Of course I did, Mr. Marshall. That's what I get paid to do."

"And my bail hearing."

"Ah yes, almost forgot. It is set for next week."

After Mr. Olanawitz left, I called Mama.

"I guess you heard by now."

"BRIAN, OH MY GOD. WHAT HAPPENED BABY. I had been waiting to hear from you ever since the story broke on the news. Your father's somewhere at the courthouse trying to find out what's going on. All that shit they saying and the way you looked, I just knew my baby was in a lot of trouble."

"Mama, none of it is true. Risha was kidnapped and me and Russell were trying to get her back. Somehow Risha wound up dead and I'm being framed for it."

"KIDNAPPED, FRAMED, DEAD, WHY DIDN'T YOU CALL THE POLICE? WHAT WERE YOU THINKING?"

"I guess I didn't think this one through too well Mama. I was worried about Risha's safety. Look you got to find Russell."

"What does Russell have to do with this?" Hold on it's your father.

"Okay, I'm back. What can we do? First of all are you okay?"

"No, I'm not okay Mama, Risha's dead." I took a deep breath. Now was not the time to lose control. We stuck to the business at hand, which was about my so-called lawyer. I expressed my doubts about his ability to represent me properly and Mama had a fit.

"What are you doing with a court appointed jerk, son? I assumed you would have hired your own attorney. Do you need me to find you a real lawyer?"

"I don't know yet Mama. I gave Mr. Olanawitz a week to get his act together but I might not have a choice in the matter. All my assets were frozen and the house is off limits being that it is a crime scene until further notice. The way I'm being railroaded, I don't think a private attorney would want to take a chance on me. You know it's money first and the possibility of them not getting paid looks pretty good."

"I have an attorney in mind and your father put away enough money for a bunch of rainy days, anything else?"

"Thanks Mama, but are you sure about this. It's going to get very expensive before it's all said and done and I still might wind up in prison."

"What we're doing is nothing compared to what you need to handle. When is your bail hearing?"

"My hearing is in a week. Look mama, Thank you, but I can't…

"Please Brian, Stop trying to do this by yourself. I'm your mother, this is what I'm supposed to do. Now stop crying in that jailhouse, I don't want anybody thinking my son is soft, although you could probably beat the whole lot of them. Make sure you call me so I can pay that bail bond." One week was all it took for me to know jail was not my type of place. The peace and quiet I craved was above and beyond what I expected. Twenty-three hours a day in a cell and one hour to stretch outside of it would drive a dead man crazy.

"Mr. Marshall, your Lawyer is here."

"Halleluiah, a visitor."

...GOOD NEWS, BAD NEWS...

"**I** LOOKED OVER YOUR case extensively Mr. Marshall and I can only come to one conclusion. We are going to take a plea if the judge will go along with it." He said plea like he had figured how to get me out of this whole mess.

"A plea deal, what kind of plea?"

"Manslaughter, Mr. Marshall."

"Manslaughter? Isn't that a confession to murder?"

"Well yes, to a lesser degree. Do you realize without a plea you go before a grand jury. If you're found guilty by said jury of your peers you could be looking at thirty to life. That's hard time for a long time. No, we are going to bargain with the judge and let him decide your fate. It shouldn't be no more than twenty which as we all know with time off for good behavior you'll probably do ten."

"Only ten, and here I was grumbling about doing a week in this godforsaken jailhouse. Has my case been investigated?" I could not hide the fact that I was more than a little annoyed at Mr. Olanawitz's assumption of my receiving a guilty verdict.

"The investigation is ongoing but early results show the deck is stacked against you."

"Well, I already knew that. That's what being framed does. You don't think you will be successful, do you?" Mr. Olanawitz pulled his chair as close to the table as his stomach would allow. With folded hands he attempted to portray the look of an important attorney instead of the soft-shelled turtle he really was who was going to read his client the riot act.

"Mr. Marshall, I am already successful, but you? You're facing a murder one charge with no witnesses in your favor. Sure we can get your family members and friends to vouch for your integrity but honestly that don't mean a thing. The dead woman was found in the trunk of your car, which you claim no memory as to what happened in the last twenty-four hours when she was killed. You obviously had a fight with her and to add insult to injury there's a video of you with some strange woman for god's sake that surfaced in the same time frame."

"Video? I don't know what you're talking about."

"You also withdrew a large sum of money from an account also around the same time period of her demise. What about that? Was that your get out of town quick money? Would you like to start over again and please, this time do not leave anything out." Other than my withdrawing that money to give to the kidnappers in exchange for Risha's life, I had no idea what he was talking about. Trying to explain to a man with a forgone conclusion that I never cheated on my wife and damn sure ain't stupid enough to put something out there to get me divorced is impossible.

"You have everything in my statement to the police and from what I told you the last time you claimed you heard every word. Judging by the way evidence and speculation was building against me, I understood why he felt like I was holding back but no matter how guilty I looked, this fool was supposed to defend me to the end. I did realize leaving Russell out of the picture was getting increasingly difficult. I remained stoic in front of Mr. Olanawitz despite my own sinking feeling of doom.

"Mr. Marshall, how can I put this? I really can't do you any good with the lack of information you're giving me. This is my first real case and it has to be with you allegedly murdering your wife who just so happens to be a popular television personality. You are very disliked right now and guilty in everybody else's eyes but your own. Do you realize the pressure that puts me under? I would like my first case to be a win."

-You know, we both can at least break even if you will agree. I will still give it my all, but the first discrepancy uncovered by the prosecuting attorney will invalidate my agreement and I will motion for a plea deal if it is still on the table."

"GIVE IT YOUR ALL? Mr. Olanawitz eyes darted toward the prison guard, his cowardly trait shining through the arrogant façade. The guard took notice and stood alert watching for the slightest hint of trouble. Dude, this is not a contest. My whole life is at stake here and all you can think about is a reputation you don't have yet. You didn't think I was innocent from the day you laid eyes on me so rather than doing your damn job to the best of your ability, a plea will still put you in the winners circle and get you a little fame in the process.

-You know what, I'd rather hire a jailhouse lawyer than to ever trust you with my case. You're fired! See your way out."

"You never hired me, Mr. Marshall but I'll be there when the judge throws the book at you, you murderer." I did a fake lunge and he cringed. The guard yelled for me to sit back down.

Mama got the call but she was two steps ahead and had gotten in touch with an old friend who was also a high powered attorney. Two days later she appeared with a tall gangly black man who began by taking care of my bail. He was dressed in a five hundred dollar suit and had a strong handshake. He put my mind at ease at first sight.

"Go to your family and take this case off your mind for awhile. I'll get back to you soon. And by the way, our trial date is set for two months from now."

"Isn't that a bit soon?"

"Yes, the powers that be want you to take the fall for this but we won't let that happen. Me and my team are already dissecting all the quote, unquote known facts of your case."

"My chances?"

"Come on Brian, Mama interrupted. Your chances are great, let William go and take care of his end."

My second day of freedom started with my having to take care of a difficult but necessary task. A knock on the door brought an unfamiliar looking Ms. Allerton to greet me in pajamas. Her swollen eyes lit up as she flew into my arms. Relieved from the belief she would add blame to the hatred she felt for me, I returned the hug before she grabbed my hand and walked into the living room. Tapping the chair back for me to sit, she continued on into the kitchen. I'd only been in her house once during my marriage for a brief visit and even then I remained in the foyer until she had gotten what Risha sent me there for and left. The house though not anywhere near as large as our home was immaculate. There were some signs of neglect mainly on Ms. Allerton herself but that was understandable considering past events. In keeping with family tradition there were plenty of pictures plastered all over the walls and furniture in expensive frames but since Risha's death the number swelled to triple the amount to include magazine and newspaper articles. Ours was a family that needed pictures to relive a moment for a pick me up when a happy memory boost was needed. She was back with a tray of coffee and cheesecake, a favorite snack of mine and then answered the look on my face.

"Risha told me some of the things you like and I made a mental note to show you I really did approve of you two, especially because you treated my baby so well. The love you had for her made me jealous and envious of my daughter. I tried and failed three times at finding a man remotely like you. Risha confided in me all the time about how you are so protective of her and that you bent over backwards to make her happy. She was fortunate to taste a little of that in her short time here. I also know you two were having problems, which is why she left the house that day. You see, she had already called me en route and said she would be staying here for a few days but she called later to say that most of the problems were her fault and that you showed her she needed to grow up.

When she was through, I filled her in from the time Risha left to the dramatic events leading up to her demise from what I knew leaving nothing out. She was quiet as she absorbed the information, putting it to rest as quickly as it was said.

"I'm glad you will be able to attend the funeral and I plan to be there for you in court also. Don't let those news reporter people get you down. I heard some of the things they were saying and that's all nonsense for them to sell papers. We chatted more about Risha and she showed me more pictures of her from birth all the way up to our wedding. I broke down completely causing the same effect from her. We grieved together for a long time before I regained enough composure to speak.

"Mother Allerton, you have no idea how much stress you have taken off of my mind." Ms. Allerton smiled.

"It was my fault you never felt secure enough to talk to me and for that I apologize. You thought to comfort me when it worried you most not knowing what to expect and that means more to me than you can know. Now, I need for you to do two things for me. Mother Allerton rose slowly from the couch and made her way to an impressive oak bookshelf sitting off in the corner of the sitting area. She picked up a thick Manila envelope and placed it in my hand as she reclaimed her seat next to me. Carry this with you tomorrow and open it when the time comes."

"When will that be?"

"Oh honey, you'll know, she said as she patted my hand. Second thing, promise you will never stop until my daughter's murderer is brought to justice."

"Mother Allerton, that's a given." That pact was a done deal made with myself a week ago.

"Good, Now you must go and prepare. Make sure you are first to arrive tomorrow so you can spend some quality time with your wife. I will make sure you are unimpeded by police or the funeral home. I need to get some sleep now so I too can look presentable tomorrow. It's going to be a big day for all of us."

"You know, they said you didn't want me anywhere near the funeral."

"Is that what they said?" I left a little happier after speaking with her. The down side was the trip down memory lane with all the pictures of Risha's life in chronological order no less. She spoke of past events, and all the little tidbits that made up a life lived. I felt more sorry for Mother Allerton than myself if that was possible because she literally lived through the exploits of her daughter. I promised myself to stay close to her during the whole funeral. Next day I got to the funeral home two hours before service and still could not beat the crowd. No one knew who was behind the tinted windows and I needed it to stay that way. Dale opened an umbrella and ushered me in before anyone could attempt to recognize me. While talking to Risha, Mother Allerton was being rushed to the hospital.

-Cause of death, overdose of sleeping pills. The announcement of her sudden demise came from the pastor at the beginning of the service. A loud gasp could be heard throughout and the minister reminded everyone that we must spend our time with Risha first and when the time comes for Mother Allerton to be buried then we will speak of her. As the minister prayed my intuition said to open the envelope right then. A notarized letter handwritten on red paper was the first thing to greet my eyes. It read: if this is the first thing you're reading from the envelope then I was right again, you do know how to open your mail, Lol. Brian, thanks to you I have the strength I needed to join my daughter. There are two things I'm comfortable with, you loved Risha unconditionally and you are going to avenge her death, this I am sure of. Now that you know I will not be there, get on that podium and read what I wrote and do not worry what anyone else has to say, you have my blessings and more important you have the lord's. Mama raised her head from prayer and moved closer to me,

"I really liked that woman, she whispered. One death has now caused another. Darn shame is what it is."

The service proceeded as normal in the standing room only church. We were in our own segregated pew where we could not be bombarded with questions or comments from any media, family or friends. I could feel the animosity directed at me and the cutting daggers from eyes wishing I was dead. It was disturbing but not overwhelming. I couldn't figure how in the world could so many minds be swayed in the direction of assuming I was guilty if they weren't there. After listening to the many friends and family members most of whom I hardly knew myself speak of their interaction in my wife's life and how they were better for the experience the pastor nodded in my direction. I stood up and as I began to approach the podium a proliferation of objectionable jeers directed at me began. The pastor quickly stepped in denouncing the rude childlike actions as un-Christian like. He for one believed I hadn't done anything wrong partly because Mother Allerton relayed that message of her belief in my innocence to him and partly because he was a good judge of character. He and I had spoken during our first meeting of pre marital counseling. He had revealed he had a good feeling that Risha picked a winner. His conviction now conveyed that to the parishioners who grew quiet with the expectation of what I had to say. I thanked the pastor, took a deep breath and began:

"I'm not here trying to elicit a change of attitude toward myself. You will think what you will think. I am here mourning the sudden loss of a loved one who was near and dear to my heart. Risha didn't belong to just me, as much as I would've liked her to but she belonged to all her adoring fans also. If there ever was an angel who walked this earth in human form, she was it. The countless ways she gave of her time away from the cameras is something very few know about. Anyone less fortunate than she who was lucky enough to cross paths went away with a smile, a full stomach, clothes, money and phone numbers for help. And yea, she also supplied them with a cell phone with which to make those important emergency calls. A member from the congregation handed me a box of tissues during one of my pauses adding a pat on my back for support.

I followed up my recollections of Risha with a neatly folded red paper Mother Allerton wanted me to read.

"This is a letter given to me by a beautiful woman I visited yesterday who I am proud to say was my mother in-law. When I finished reading, a standing ovation ensued as I placed it back in the envelope and went to my seat. Happy the majority of the church had been swayed in the belief of my innocence, it was a very sad occasion nonetheless.

As the time got near I insisted on being up on the stand when the trial started and William was adamant in his answer each time, which was a definite, NO. He did urge me into talking with the press in an attempt at quelling all the stories floating around. I felt good about my chances since turning a whole funeral congregation in my favor so I agreed to it. I didn't want my face plastered all over the tube where I would be more recognizable than I already was so William had make up artists alter my look somewhat. At a predetermined place the deluge of idiocy began.

Reporter#1- "Did you kill Mrs. Allerton dead because she discovered you cheating on her with said unnamed prostitute on the video that went viral?"

Brian- "Well, I never cheated on my wife. Where did you get that from?"

Reporter#2- "Is it true Risha Allerton cheated to get back at you for cheating and you killed her in a jealous fit?"

Brian, "Cheated on me, Risha?"

Reporter#3- "Is there a love child and where is he?" The floodgates were now open and nothing was taboo. The media like relentless dogs were untiring in their ruthless pursuit of my business. The problem was most of their information was rumors they either believed or wanted confirmed. The truth was a joke no one wanted to hear because it's unappealing and therefore no money is in the truth. Two, three, four absurd questions at a time were fired at me. When I stumbled over my words I'd hear an aha like I just confessed by accident. By the time William intervened just about everything I said had been taken out of context. He shut down the flood of questions with one statement.

"Mr. Marshall has nothing more to say at this time. There will be a statement addressing all questions in the near future."

"There will?" I asked as he whisked me away from the horde of reporters.

"And that's why I don't want you to take the stand. Defense attorneys are trained to do a far better job of breaking you down than those nosey ass reporters are." Two days later I was prepped to go on air with my exclusive three minute message.

"Listen, the director spoke as makeup did their altering techniques. This is live, meaning one shot. You have to be sad, but not pitiful. Do not go off script, plenty of eye contact to the camera and keep your hands on the podium. As you know by now we are not trying to give them any more ammunition than what they already have. When I hold up two fingers, you have two minutes. I will then hold up one, where you should be wrapping it up. It's easy, just speak from your heart and make them believe." I shook my head,

"Yea easy.

"This is a sad occasion for all of us but for me I have to endure the grief of never seeing my wife again. There are many doubters to my being innocent, which only adds to the torment I have to endure while trying to absolve myself of all guilt. Risha and myself shared a bond, which only in death was broken. We had our problems like any other couple but hate was not one of them. If anything, I am guilty of loving her too much which drove her away but also brought her back. She was kidnapped and murdered and believe me, I want to get to the bottom of this as much as any loving husband would. I am working with the police and I feel certain they will use every tool at their disposal to solve this case and exonerate me." Out of the corner of my eye I could see the director's unwavering finger.

"Time to wrap it up," He mouthed.

"No questions will be answered until all the facts are in. Thank you for listening and please let's revere her memory, and not her murder." The Director held a thumbs up for a good speech. It was a relief to explain myself without the press botching up my answers. It didn't matter though, assumptions were made and stuck to and irrefutable proof would be needed to make an ass out of the naysayers.

My one saving grace was the world still focused the brunt of attention on Risha from childhood to star. The love/hate relationship viewers had with her alter ego vixen, Monique was reminiscent of an epic saga surely to be turned into a movie some day. I shook my head at the insanity of it all. It is true, the more tragic the death, the more popular you become. Overnight she became bigger than her name. Fan club sites popped up on the net along with the hunger to devour everything with her name attached to it. Perfume stamped Monique', a clothing line, x rated pictures super imposed with her face, the list went on and on. Her soap opera enjoyed their highest ratings yet when her scenes appeared, which would continue until the end of the season. New followers across the world became addicted to her show and were up in arms to put away the piece of shit that silenced her forever.

Russell sat naked amidst the squalor that surrounded him, his address the only change in a miserable existence. Premature arthritic fingers probed scarred legs hoping to get lucky as he, undeterred moved to the inside of his thighs, in the end deciding on a large vein that ran the length of his penis. Strapping it the same way he would do his arm, the object of his desire protruded against the inside layer of skin. It would not prove easy for a limp penis to remain still enough to be punctured. It moved as though aware of the outside force attacking it but Russell having experience in this region of the anatomy pulled his penis tight to pinpoint where the needle will penetrate. With three failed attempts at spearing the elusive vein, success and the reward of another drug induced nirvana.

Hopes of starting anew with the stolen money went down the drain with his first high that same fateful night. Mink had hung around long enough to relieve him of all of it and vanished. Damian was disappointed but not surprised in Russell's failure believing it was inconceivable that a junkie could make a sound plan when it came to stealing on a higher scale and Russell was proof positive. Damian added Russell and family to his calendar of to do's. Their deaths would serve as a warning against any more foolish acts of thievery within his organization. A contract issued on the remaining three family members minus Russell was to be enforced right after the verdict. Russell wasn't worth a bullet but more significantly he gets to witness what he set in motion. Russell swore he'd kill Mink when the chance arrived but in the meantime he was due for another hit and no money. His brother came to mind, he could talk to him, get back on his good side, after all blood is thicker than water. On the other hand his brother got arrested and a lock was put on all things pertaining to money.

...A MOTHER'S LOVE...

IN THE BACK of my mind resided the hope that Russell would be found alive so I could get to the answer of really happened when I passed out. What I really believed was we were double crossed, he got into a fight he could not win and he and the woman were killed. My trial date was a week away and I heard nothing new. Everyone it seemed was in a holding pattern until court was in session and the guilty verdict came out. I myself compulsively hit the redial. It was time to tell William why Risha was kidnapped.

"William, any news yet?"

"Nothing since the last time I heard from you which I believe was five minutes ago. Relax son, you will be the first person I call when there is something to call about."

"I need to tell you something about the case."

"Son, believe me when I tell you it's under control. There's nothing you need to tell me and stop your worrying, between me and your parents you are in good hands. When the world as you know it has crashed, any help in your survival is not only appreciated but you become that itch under your savior's skin.

While William's detective finished digging up answers to the questions that weren't asked, Mama was focused on her own detecting. She told William to let her take care of the missing link to the case, namely her son. She hoped that Russell was just as innocent a pawn in all this as I was, but she had a sneaking suspicion this was not the case. Finding someone on the streets is, unless you know their pattern of habits is like looking for a needle in a haystack. She knew Russell and that meant it wouldn't be easy but not impossible. She had to return back from where she came and immerse herself into an environment that was unfavorable to the average person. Weeks of consistent hard core junkie to dealer searching rewarded her with quite a few close calls. She was not of their kind any longer and the vibes from the fallen was evident in their reactions. If it wasn't for the looming figure of her husband the possibilities of being robbed, raped or killed were very likely. He never completely showed himself until necessary but when he did that meant there was a problem that had to be dealt with. He looked like his old self when he knocked around a couple of thugs who wanted Mama to give them all her money. There was a reminiscent flood of good memories when she saw him fight which transferred to the bedroom late at night. End of the second week she was informed after Pop coerced a young man who was stupid enough to figure them for easy prey where Russell could be found. He lived on the outskirts of town with a new set of cohabitants. She knocked herself in the head, should've figured that out long ago. She told her husband to go home and let her handle this. He agreed to be nearby but he was not going home without her.

"RUSSELL, Mama called out as she stumbled around all of the drug engorged bodies of men and women laying haphazardly everywhere. Looks like dawn of the dead up in here," she mumbled to herself, with her eyes darting this way and that. She remembered her youth and the times she had to bed down among these very same types. As long as they were high they were no more dangerous than a flower blowing in the breeze. Looking at the shape of this group of souls in here was making her stomach churn which was not easy for a woman who had seen man at his worst many times. She prayed Russell was in better shape than these young people in this room. The small powerful halogen flashlight she carried spotlighted a barely recognizable skeletal figure of a naked man sitting in a corner of a second room.

"Russell baby is that you?" She had to be sure. A check of a birthmark clinched it and her heart sank. Russell had shrunk to double-digit pounds with maggots feeding in the gaping sores covering what little flesh was left. The stench of death made it just about impossible to breathe but Mama paid that no mind.

"Oh baby, I didn't know the devil had such a grip on your earthly body. He was in such a bad state it was obvious he didn't have long for this world. Russell was in a deep nod at the moment until mama shook him into a semi responsive state. With teary eyes she sat on the filthy excrement stained floor and gathered his frail body in her arms. She hugged him like a mother who loves her son, saddened by the vision of him deep in this hellish misery. From the bottom of my heart I am sorry for not being there when you needed me most. Russell was quiet while tears trickled down his face that let Mama know he was listening. They talked quietly amid the blight in that crowded apartment as if it was just the two of them. She finally got to the point of her being there.

"Son, Your brother is in a lot of trouble. It seems everybody is against him and he can't see his way clear. If any wrong was done to him by you, here's your chance to set it right." Russell's eyes lit up as he jumped at the chance to explain his role in the set up. With a voice no stronger than a whisper he fought to be heard.

"Mama, it wasn't supposed to go down like that. I love Brian. The best thing that ever happened in my whole life was being the best man at his wedding." Mama sat with him for the better part of an hour recording all the sordid details of his betrayal. They cried together and then apologized to each other again. The purge was something of a liberation for each. Mama needed to make sure Russell's heavy laden soul was spiritually blessed and that he knew, she as well as God had forgiven him of all his sins. Russell needed to know Mama loved him and he was truly sorry for what he did to me as well as her. She was glad she came.

"Mama, I don't want to do this anymore."

"Shhh, I know baby, I know. Don't you worry, Mama's here. I'm going to get you some help." Russell shook his head as he spoke in halted sentences between bouts of severe cramps.

"It's too late for that kind of help Mama. Look at me, I'm being eaten alive and I'm too weak to stop it." He spoke of his inflictions, hepatitis, aids, rheumatoid arthritis and the misery of being two thirds dead. Mama let him talk, get it out of his system so he'll change his mind. She rocked slowly as she listened the way she did when he was a toddler. Russell's pleas had not gone unnoticed but still she begged for him to let her find another way. They prayed and prayed and then he was quiet. Not the quiet of finished talking but the quiet of eternal rest. This, her visit is what he'd been waiting for. She held him as she shed tears for Pop, as she cried for her other son, as she cried for herself and most of all she cried for tears of joy in celebration of Russell's absolution. She realized with painful clarity what needed to be done next and vengeance shall be mine, she whispered.

She stepped outside and pressed redial, as she had done a million times but this time it was different. Great sadness enveloped her at the unexpected turn of events that invaded her family's life. It is not over with yet, she thought as she asked her husband to please come and get her. True to his overprotective nature, he was only a few blocks away, always ready, always at her beck and call some twenty plus years later. She jumped in the car, the despair inescapable to his keen sense and knowledge of his wife.

"You okay," he asked already knowing the answer.

"I will be. He stopped at a red light and she leaned over and kissed him tenderly. I love you so very much."

"Ditto," he answered taking the word from their favorite movie. He didn't ask about Russell and she never volunteered. It was just as well to leave things as they were. He was in God's hands now.

...IT'S A NEW DAY...

TWO DAYS PRIOR to the beginning of the case William called.

"Can you come in today?" His exuberance didn't escape me.

"It sounds like you have good news," I said finding it contagious.

"Just come in, I'll explain it all when you get here." The news was better than expected. The case was close to being thrown out because of quite a few discrepancies dug up by two detectives, one I found to be my mother. The irrefutable proof showed most of what I had claimed was true. Certain loose ends had to be tied up which would seal the unemployment of some key figures in the department. The supposed video produced on me wanted people to believe I was cheating on my wife and to give the impression that I probably killed her when she discovered I had a mistress. The rest of the story is easy to figure out. The video was so bad it is inadmissible because both adults are unrecognizable. Her face is hidden intentionally and his face is covered in blackness. It was found that I did have drugs in my system, the type that made me an unwilling though very viable participant. William gave me a look of uncertainty.

"There's more and this part is not good. I'm glad you are sitting down son. -We have the name of the person who allegedly framed you and murdered your wife."

"You're kidding? Who?"

"I'm sorry to say, it was your brother." Shocked couldn't begin to describe the look on my face. My whole demeanor changed, first being disbelief.

"Are you sure, my brother Russell?"

"I'm afraid so and it doesn't stop there." Before I can try to understand William's first bombshell, he wants to impart more.

"Slow down William. Let this sink in for a minute before you go trying to ruin the rest of my life. I took a deep breath and tried to put things in order. So my brother lied to my face after killing the love of my life Risha for which I was persecuted for by the police, the press and her peers for what, money?" The lawyer shook his head as he repeated only what was told to him.

"The murder was accidental as was the kidnapping once he saw how much of an impact it had on you."

"Really, what did he expect it to have? And me being framed, wasn't that premeditated. Never mind, so where is he now, in custody?"

"Well no, he's at the morgue and your mother is in custody being questioned. -Or she is for the next sixty minutes or so."

"Seriously, are you shitting me? WHY, in the world would they arrest my mother?"

"It seems your mother was with him when he took his last breath. You still have time to catch her." With five minutes to spare, I spotted mama speaking with a court officer.

"Damn you look like you're running from a ghost, son. What's up? I know you heard the news you about to be a free man."

"Never mind that Mama, Please tell me what the hell is going on."

"I knew that ol' big mouth William would say something. He's not going to ever change. You wasn't supposed to see me here. I was going to call and tell you about all that happened but these policemen had me jumping through hoops with all the questions and processing and everything. Can you believe they making me see a shrink to see if I'm mentally stable? Last time I saw a shrink I was eighteen. For a quick second Mama had that faraway look while she relived some memory of the good old days except as told by her, they didn't get good until after she met Pop. Shoot boy, don't you worry, your mama's free and clear of all charges." Mama was smiling and acting different.

"Honey, there's major changes taking place in our lives. Listen up because it's very important you understand me. Mama gave me a five minute synopsis on her visit with Russell and how important it was that I forgive him and have him buried with a proper funeral. Then the bombshell dropped about Pop was dying from some type of rare brain disease. It was in a progressive state disintegrating his brain cells rapidly as we speak. He was on some kind of medicine that slows the cell destruction down a bit, but becoming a vegetable was imminent. He had about two months tops to get his business in order before the degeneration completed its disastrous effects. Tears rolled down my cheeks for the millionth time as I listened. Mama hugged me, surprised I had any tears left to cry. You know, the doctor had to break his promise not to tell me what's going on because your father didn't want his problem to take precedence over yours. I tell you, you two drove poor William crazy tag phoning him every day. Even now you know that old fool's worried sick over my being in here. I figured a nice weeklong retreat with some serious lovemaking and snuggling should make him feel better. What do you think son?"

"Yea Mama, That sounds fine.

-But Mama…" Mama stood and pulled me up with her.

"Brian, life has its pitfalls and potholes. We have to endure the bad times so we can enjoy the good times for as long as they last. This is a bad time so rejoice, good times are right around the corner. I love you baby, now go. Your father will be here any minute and I don't need you spoiling our reunion. We will call you when we return." Here I am, devastated and Mama took everything in stride like it was just another pothole. Yea it's a good idea we get together later, the fear of my breaking down if I saw him was absolute.

I walked away with my mind wading through an ocean of scenes from a life that was destroyed. One thing was for sure, now that It's lost do I realize how good my life really was.

"Lord forgive me, I know you never give us more than we can handle." I said it, more than once but in my heart I didn't believe it, then I went into the nearest liquor store. One fifth of scotch and an all night binge took my mind off of the problems of the present.

William called soon after I got in. Five rings of bone jarring noise before voicemail picked up. Blocking the noise is futile but the tightly wrapped pillow doubles as a support to prevent my head from falling on the floor. Suicide takes a quick run through my mind since revenge is no longer an option but I'm too sick to entertain the thought. My voicemail answers the latest round of rings. It's information pertaining to the case and my future.

Eight a.m. along with a thousand or so onlookers we're at the courthouse. After the judge settled everyone down he asked for the opening statements. The prosecutor looked over his paperwork and stood up.

"Your honor, members of the jury, citizens of New York. In light of recent new evidence discovered, the state of New York withdraws its case against Brian Marshall." There was an instant uproar as the media began transmitting news all over the country. The judge hammered his gavel several times calling for order so he could give his two cents and it wasn't good.

"The discrepancies discovered are appalling for a department that prides itself in fair treatment to all. This case was solved because of the due diligence of the suspect's mother and hired outside help. The sloppiness and intentional disregard of the evidence is the real crime here and it is unacceptable. Take notice, all those involved officers and detectives involved in this heinous cover up will be facing departmental charges pending an investigation. Mr. Marshall, It is with my deepest apologies you had to endure this travesty of justice in your time of extreme crisis. I hope that now, you can mourn in peace. With a hard smack of the gavel the judge thanked the jury and shouted dismissed. The murder case that had the entire world sitting on pins and needles waiting for some kind of fantastic outcome did not disappoint thanks to the judge. There were no smiles, no jumps of joy, only the awareness that I now go home to an empty house and be reminded of what was. Now the pain of loss of my whole family really takes hold.

Pop and Mama video conferenced me from wherever they were vacationing. They had another surprise waiting for me after we talked at length about getting Pop the best doctors in the world. Me and Pop talked more over the internet than in all the years I'd known him but it was nothing I didn't know. He loved me and was always there for me for anything without question. Mama explained I would be receiving an e-mail from them on certain things that needed attending to because they would not be coming home again. I beg and plead until the face to face connection is severed and we use our phones. I know it was intentional so I settle for living in the moment, fleeting as it is, knowing I will never see these two great people ever again. I hint it's not too late, there is enough money to try and find a possible cure no matter where it might be. They laugh and call me a soldier but truth of the matter was, it was too late for Pop and Mama swore her life to him. I asked about burial plans, funerals and such. Everything was taken care of. I try to keep them on the phone as long as possible but that time came and went and yet I needed more time. I ignore that beep my phone makes when it warns me of a dying battery, praying that it understands how important it is to give me more than what it has. Pop says his phone is about dead also but God keeps his word and we say the type of goodbyes needed, filled with the deep love and adoration we felt for each other. In keeping up with the dramatic way of doing things my parents went on a cruise and jumped overboard in the dead of night handcuffed to each other. I got the news of their suicide one week later. The news was what I expected yet it still hit me hard. Later that day I had that nervous breakdown that I fought so hard not to get and was rushed to the hospital. Pop and Mama had left me a long e-mail marked for my eyes only. They, by the way were never found.

...WORK TO FORGET...

OUT OF THE hospital with a clean bill of health, I ignore my doctor's prescription for Prozac because I know what's needed to bring me back to my old self. The gym looks inviting and I get right to it. The old feel of my body expanding beyond its normal limits to accommodate an outside force captivates me. I have an audience fascinated as well over my intense focus so they watch. A subtle move of my head and my self appointed helpers add iron to the bar. I push myself to near exhaustion, more weights, more reps, no outside thoughts, I feel free. The sweat I expel is mixed with the poisons of a painful year. When the cleansing is complete I will know. Four times a week for months I repeat this procedure until one day I scream. I scream until my throat is dry and my tonsils swell. A tall glass of water finishes the process.

Home isn't home for me, only a place to lay my head. I moved from the old neighborhood trying to run from familiar and yet I brought it with me. My place is right off of 150th, on the twenty-first floor. It was a nice fit to my personality. Up and coming hard working middle class families not into the gossipy, nosy neighbor shit. Leave me alone, I leave you alone kind of thinking. I log onto my computer, it opens with a sexy picture of Risha on my desktop and I click on a folder downloaded from my e-mail labeled M-and-P. I take a deep breath, a taste of scotch and wait for the slow burn of the liquid to dissipate before reading. It starts off with Hello from Mom and Pop. It's a long video, plenty to be said for the final conversation of your life. There were no sad stories, they knew I had enough to deal with including losing them. They clung to each other, still inseparable from the first day fate put them together. I was glad they had found each other, not for my sake, they like anyone else deserved some happiness after such a rough beginning. For a moment they were in the room with me while we laughed at a joke together. I wipe an escaped teardrop as I shut it down leaving with a promise of returning tomorrow to finish our time together. This is something you can't rush, it's a conclusion of the life between us and I need to live it with them.

The next morning I take delight in more of the same from my e-mail. Those two took a million selfies, insurance I will never forget. Towards the end Mama got serious when she imparted important information from her investigation. I now had a reason why Russell did what he did. He gave Mama a partial name but the mystery woman he was with that fateful night might be able to supply me with the rest of the story. My heart quickened in anticipation of where my reawakening will take me. Someone had blood on their hands for causing Risha's death and their blood would soon be on mine. There was no better time than the present and I couldn't wait to get filthy again but now as a willing participant. I shut my laptop off. Her name escaped me but that didn't matter, she being my only link left of the whole unfortunate kidnap fiasco, had to be found. I got on the phone right away and got hold of William. The situation was explained and he would get back to me. Last I remember she was an addict which means finding her won't be easy. Who's to say she's not completely out of her mind by now or worse, dead. I needed to try. Everyday the killer of my wife got to breath air he no longer deserves and he had to be killed. The detective hit the streets starting at the bottom of the gutter. In two days he found himself at the top of an apartment complex in the Bronx. Mink had managed to kick her habit and moved on up a bit.

"Hello, Is this Mink?" I asked certain that the number I received from the detective was correct. Mink's heart went to her throat. She knew who it was the second she picked up, but regained enough control of herself to answer.

"Who wants to know?" came a cautious reply.

"This is Brian, Russell's brother. Remember me?" I smiled knowing she was very much surprised. Mink was more than surprised, she was scared. Had her past caught up with her? She always knew it was only a matter of time.

"Yes Brian, I remember you. How did you get my number?"

"I have my ways. You sound well."

"I owe that to one year clean, but I'm sure you didn't hunt me down just to hear my voice so what do I owe this phone call to?"

"If you don't mind can we meet somewhere and talk. I need to clear up a few things."

"I don't mind but what makes you think I am the person you need to speak with."

"You was in the house when I passed out. I'm not going to take up too much of your time. Brunch or dinner is on me."

"Okay, sure, give me a date and time and I'll rearrange my schedule."

"If it's convenient, now would be fine if you're not busy." She agreed in an hour.

"I guess I don't need to tell you where I live."

"Got it right here." I grabbed one of my many handguns I now collected for just in case reasons, you can't trust anyone these days.

One knock and a voice shouts from the other side to come on in, it's unlocked. I enter expecting a small cheaply furnished apartment, instead I am standing in a spacious well decorated living room. Inside contradicted the appearance of the dilapidated looking exterior. I wondered if the rest of the buildings inhabitants could boast the same. I wasn't into decorating, that was Risha's thing but I did manage to absorb some of her craft. Mink's taste in pictures for one thing would be in Risha's eyes, diverse, offbeat and dramatic. I say this because the first thing that stares you in the face long before you look at the rest of her collection is a huge picture of painted eyes in a Picasso type likeness. There were more colorful paintings with crazy splashes thrown in for no reason other than the artist felt it was needed. Her furniture likened to the more comfortable modern type except for the two antique stools sitting on either end of her s-shaped coffee table. Everything looked new, like yesterday's sale.

Her entrance is designed to be dramatic and she succeeds with her white business revealing attire. The modified mini suit with a push up bra to show off more of her large breasts was unnecessary but attention getting. I did not remember what she looked like at our first meeting other than she had reminded me of someone strung out. I am looking at a woman who I can see, wants my acknowledgement of her beauty. I don't give it to her but I do realize the ache I have for a woman in my arms although she is not it and I remind her I'm here on business only. She understands but doesn't change so I dismiss it and we leave. By the time we arrive at Angelo's for dinner she had informed me that she and Russell parted ways that same night.

"I felt bad about Russell's murder. I'm so sorry and especially for your mom. It's got to be some deep stuff to hold your dying son as he fades away. Her hand rested on my hand as she spoke, something that wasn't lost on me. I nodded my agreement reclaiming my hand as I did.

"Why is it you were never mentioned by Russell for being a participant in my wife's kidnapping and murder."

"Well Brian, You know I was as much a victim as you were. Your brother threatened to kill me and my daughter if I didn't do exactly as he said."

"And that is?"

"You really don't know much do you," Mink said as she studied me like a hawk.

"Nah, nobody's said much except for all the tall tales the media has spun."

"Mink's mind went into storytelling mode now. She had practiced her lies over and over in case the police ever questioned her but this, Let's just say this tall tale is a masterpiece in the making.

"Sip your coffee slow and relax Brian, I will spell the whole thing out for you."

She and Russell met many years ago buying drugs from the same dealer. They became fast friends then partners as a team robbing Johns. After a while she developed a habit of her own and wanted to keep one hundred per cent of her take. The partnership dissolved with Russell going his own way and for years their paths stayed separate. Somehow Russell found her and called about this plan to rob me. He told her it was foolproof but he couldn't do it alone. When it was found out he was robbing his own flesh and blood she wanted no parts of it. He said it was too late and that he had no time to change her mind so precautions had been taken. Her daughter would be used to make certain she was a participant. She had no choice but to do whatever was asked of her. Her job was to pick up the money at the drop off and then he would come five minutes after that and drop my wife off. When she got to the apartment he ordered her to sit down and wait. I was spellbound as I listened to the moments of my life being transformed into the grotesque facsimile of what it was today.

"How did Risha get into my trunk?"

"I don't know, so let me finish."

"Sorry, go on. You had just walked into the apartment and…"

"And I could hear Russell talking at someone in the other room. The woman sounded angry and said I know it's you Russell and then she screamed. I heard him hit her so I went running to see what happened. Your woman had blood all over her, so I tried to clean her up. I think he cut her but I'm not sure. Russell warned me if I interfered again I would be next, then my daughter. He told me to get my ass back in the other room and close the door. After a minute or two he came out of the room with her pocketbook in hand looking for money. He sent me out to cop while he put the fear of Russell into her, his words. When I got back everything was quiet and he told me there was a change in plans and to help carry your wife to the car. I don't think she was dead then but I don't really know. He made me drive to your house and come inside. After you were drugged he told me he would take it from there and to go get my daughter. I'm sorry I never said anything but I was so scared I just put it out of my mind. I hope this is helpful."

"The mysterious video that popped up on the net of me and some woman?"

"Is that really you? I saw it on the Internet too 'and it looked like a fake. Anyway, I don't remember seeing Russell with a video camera, of course I could be wrong."

"I need to know about this gangster Russell sold drugs for. The mere mention of this person showed in the fear on her face. That bastard had beaten her within an inch of her young life during the short period she was involved with him. If she had stayed with him any longer she would not be sitting here today eating this great meal and enjoying the money stolen from under Russell's nose.

"I sense some kind of ill will between you two."

"No, just a very bad memory that's all. What do you want to know about him?"

"Everything." The mention of this one name, of a person she had not seen in years changed her whole upbeat attitude. He still had a tight hold on her mentally but my issue with him had nothing to do with what she was dealing with and quite frankly I didn't care. She was despondent as all the gory details that were Damian came to light. After she finished and I was satisfied, I tried to lighten the mood.

"Dinner with an attractive woman should never end on a sour note. So, tell me how did you manage to free yourself from your addiction?"

"Well, I found the spiritual guidance necessary to change my weakness and value myself more. I have since used my past life experiences to become a successful motivational speaker." I had to admit, this was not the story I expected to hear. My next question was how long had she and my brother been an item? She denounced that piece of information with a firm never.

"We were friends with a common goal," was her reply. Mink smiled. I'm glad we talked."

"Oh, why is that, I asked."

"Ever since I kicked, this whole Russell thing has been the last terrible item I needed to clear in my life so I can be truly free of my past. I know it doesn't do much for you but thank you anyway." I left that evening feeling a little different about her. I expected to see her one way but instead I received an entirely different picture of who she was. She wasn't a bad person at all. At the very least, justice was served even if it was my brother. I received a surprise call from Mink the next day saying she had more information to divulge. I showed up in time for a dinner I believe was being cooked especially for me.

"I hope you're hungry," Mink asked from her location at the stove. Roast or chicken, she handed me a knife and fork to do the cutting.

At dinners end I pressed her for the extra bit of information she had promised and got instead the other side of Mink, the woman who was a pro at seducing men. We sat on the couch with me making sure a sizable gap stood between us. She took the liberty of bridging said gap when a problem arose with a speck of dirt invading her eye. After the problem was solved and before I knew what hit me she wasn't talking anymore, instead her lips had found mine and were devouring me. She gave me no time to protest as my body was attacked in a lustful onslaught designed to feed my need for sexual release. I hadn't had this strong an urge since Risha and with all the shit I went through and still going through, I, as they say didn't have a chance in hell. An internal battle raged within me but her mind was made up and she would not be denied. This is one time I lost the fight. Once Mink knew I was game she pulled out all the stops. Throw taboo out the window as nothing was off limits to her pleasure hunt. My erogenous zones became an open portal, bowing to her every whim until she slipped me a small blue pill, said to trust her and so I did. I felt a simmering fire within me grow to a blazing inferno. My senses were intensified and I became super sensitive to every touch. Nothing mattered except the climax that I knew would be spectacular. Mink didn't disappoint. She made certain my ride to relief was nothing less than phenomenal. Satisfied, sleep came quick and lasted for ten hours with me waking up a new man. I found Mink in the kitchen making coffee. I wanted to know what the pill was she had given me.

"Just a little something to take you to a higher level, did it do the job?"

"That and more."

"Again tomorrow I hope?"

"How can I say no." Like clockwork I showed up at her door everyday for two weeks. The times were different but the same mind blowing experience was the same. I was amazed at the passionate intensity this woman exhibited. It almost felt like a spell was being cast on me and I was helpless to fight it. Mink left me a voicemail today. It's been two days since I've seen her and I never thought I would say this, but I could use the rest.

The following week it all started again. The woman was lying on the bed wearing the sheerest of negligees. She asked was I there as a spectator or as a participant. She looked good in red, I chose participant. It's a wonder, the depths evil can go and how beauty can cause you to not see it even if it's staring you in the face. All of that feeling displayed by her was part of a scheme. After our lovemaking and while she lay hugged up enjoying the afterglow I decided to inform her of my need for us to go our separate ways.

"Mink, I think you are a strong, beautiful woman inside and out. If things weren't so messed up we could have a go of a relationship. But now is not the time so this will have to be our last time together." I stroked her arm lightly praying that the news didn't have too much of a bad impact on her.

"Thank you for such a sweet thought but what I have to say might make you want to retract that statement. Look Brian, I'm going to get right to the point. I need two hundred thousand dollars from you." I got out of the bed.

"What the hell are you talking about?"

"I'm talking rape, Brian. You raped me and I'm about to get hysterical to a 911 operator if I don't get a signed check from you." She held the phone out for my attention.

"You can't be serious. So everything you did was a setup. You're still just a stupid crackhead out of her league."

"Wrong, I'm not a crackhead. But yea, this was a setup and I wanted to see if you could fuck better when you were awake."

"I'll be damned, you the bitch in the video. Call the cops and while you're at it, get you a good lawyer cause I ain't giving your nasty ass shit."

"YOU think I'm fucking with you. Remember the knife you used to cut the roast with, the one with your fingerprints all over it, I saved it. I'm sure you can figure out where the doctor will find your DNA so don't test me, I already got away with murder so fucking up what little bit of life you have left won't be any trouble."

"Who'd you murder Mink?" It was a calm request, meant to sound ignorant on my part and to keep her fearless as she bragged.

"There's nothing you can do about it now. Still think I'm out of my league?"

"Okay, I can't do nothing about it so who did you murder?"

"You know who, your precious Monique' when I shoved my knife into her ass. The sound of her cell phone crashing against the wall from my kick was nothing in comparison to her utter disbelief of what was next to come. Mink's bulging eyes translated her terror welling up from a death grip cutting off any hint of oxygen relief forcing her mouth to open and close mirroring a fish sucking for something that was not there. Devoid of any humanity, I tightened my hold on this monster pretending to be a human.

"My wife's name was Risha you stupid bitch." Mink dropped to the floor in a lifeless heap ignored for the moment while sanity reclaimed my senses. My thought centered on how do I explain this after my acquittal of Risha and like Mink said irrefutable proof that we were together.

Yes judge, I killed her because she admitted something you assholes should have known from the beginning instead of throwing me under the bus. Nah, the foregone conclusion is she deserved to die and if I had it to do over the outcome would be the same. My decision made, there remained the task of removing the evidence. It became clear Russell's kidnap attempt turned into a frame all due to this bitch he knew was delusional when he left her alone with Risha. Why he never implicated Mink is anyone's guess mine being it would not have mattered, no one would have believed him except Mama. Why didn't he tell Mama, I wondered.

I got busy trying to erase all traces of my being in her presence. There was no blood to contend with, which as any murderer can attest, is a pain in the ass to conceal and in this day and age is damn near impossible. With the missing knife found, my plan was to slip out sometime during the AM when most were asleep. Once this mess is over, I will leave anything that has Russell's name attached to it behind. Too much bad karma associated with him.

A laptop lay partially hidden under the bed begging for some attention. No password and a folder named JIC on the desktop caught my eye. One click on it opened up a world of some fucked up shit. (JUST IN CASE) was a file on murders from years back until now and planned future hits. Included were Robberies, rackets and drug operations with names and addresses behind them. It made for interesting reading until I came across four names that as it turns out forced Mink to push up her timetable on that blackmail scheme. There were strikes through three of them and the fourth was due in one week. If this wasn't enough of a surprise, she too was on Damian's hit list for being part of the reason of Russell's failure. It appears Damian was apprised of our every encounter in the hopes of having me set up and her obligations forgiven, instead she was ordered to take care of the hit. A new plan formed when a check of the address book turned up a Damian Woods. Three-ten Lawrence Rd., It was an apartment building with an attached storefront.

...DATE NIGHT....

IT'S BEEN A few hours since Mink's demise. The sun was giving way to my favorite time of day. Long ghoulish shadows cast off bodies in sync with the dropping daylight as if to forewarn of impending doom. On these streets, safety conscious residents retreated to the shelter of home behind triple locked doors and pulled shades. Vicious representatives from hell are awakened like vampires from a good days rest, drawing their energy from a bright moon painted on a darkened sky. They set out to leave their mark of terror on unsuspecting victims unlucky enough cross their path. The seventy-five degree heat of the day will be replaced with falls nighttime fifty, perfect weather for a workout. My outfit was picked with the pretense of preparing for our grand debut. A clean white tee, pressed black jeans topped off with a black cotton jacket complete my ensemble and as you can tell it's a casual come as you are event. The guest of honor is wearing a gas soaked robe looking ready, as she will ever be for her debut as well. In the backseat were three gallon plastic containers leaking fluid through all the holes poked in them forming a pool on the floor. A picture of Damian sat on her lap ready to burn in effigy like it has burned its way in my memory. No sooner was the match thrown, a spectacular flame shot up to the sky burning bright as it swiftly consumed someone else's vehicle who by now I hope filed a claim. It took three minutes before the fire licked with their red hot flames at the gas tank rupturing it and causing a thunderous explosion.

"Now that's the difference between diamond and glass," I said to no one as I shook my head in approval at the shattered windows in the building.

In the shadows I lurked, confident that in the ensuing confusion Damian will exit, only to die by my hands. Four dazed young men ran out, each deciding on his own haphazard direction to flee. Damian is not one of them so the unlucky one who came the closest, got snatched in mid-stride and slammed against the building. He looked about seventeen with the face of a kid who knows he's guilty of something. His eyes are like saucers as the pleas of 'don't kill me' spilled out before I could open my mouth. I caught on quick, the fire with its dancing flames lighting up parts of me cast a sinister view of my face spooking the boy. Any other time it would be funny but now funny is something I have no taste for. There's no ill will between us but I do need some questions answered so his fear will be my choice of tools as long as he does nothing stupid. Where's Damian is the first question he's asked while being held in a tight hold with a thumb pushing into his eye. He's an instant chatterbox, answering all questions asked and unasked.

Mink's place had been wired with cameras in every room so Damian watched the whole episode unfold before him. Shortly thereafter he received a message from an informant that the feds were closing in. Always prepared for this moment, his immediate departure for Florida was the first stop where his headquarters would be transitioned to foreign soil. The kid knew nothing about what the message consisted of but he and the other three kids were supposed to take me out in the interim with a promise that they get the money offered from the hit.

He is reassured that the interest in my hurting him is not there but he needs to find something else to do with his time. Damian will kill him if he leaves he tells me with the remorsefulness of wishing he never made this huge mistake. Here's my card, I tell him to call me if his friends have a problem with his leaving but Damian, let's just say he's got bigger problems than one less gang member. I let him go to run and catch up with his buddies so he can figure out what to do. There is a sea of people out trying to determine what the cause and effect this new commotion means to the neighborhood. I keep walking in the direction of home to pack, looks like I'll be heading south tomorrow.

...BLACK ANGELS...

WILLIAM KNEW THE call was important but Sharon was not the type of woman that would be placed in a holding pattern while he took care of job related matters. She always made it worth his while to ignore all things not her and this time was no exception. At the first ring, her hand took command of his manhood, the move calculated to give her the edge against a strong sense of duty to his clients. Hers was a match William looked for in the hundreds of women he dated throughout the years. Her dominance in the home offset his dominance in business, something she took no interest in. Enemies have evolved since the good old days of run and gun so in taking the old saying to heart, when someone is too good to be true, it's probably a set-up so he took no chances. Sharon being the smart woman she was figured out in routine conversation he had her investigated, confronted him on it and then agreed with his actions when her suspicions were confirmed. It was a match made in heaven going forward.

In the morning, messages missed were at the top of Williams to do list. My call was first and it was the only call he didn't like missing. William I had learned was a man of many means and being a damn good attorney was the only above board legal one. His office layout was typical for a successful practice, impressive oak desks that sat on a wall to wall plush black carpet featuring phones ringing off the hook with men and women scurrying back and forth on missions of mercy for those in need of counsel. Two huge blackboards hung on opposite walls surrounded by eight by ten and eleven by fourteen framed pictures chosen by the Para-legals themselves, chalked up with reminders, need to knows, names, places of relevance etc., also attached magnets holding local delivery numbers of restaurants, flyers, and on and on. Open cabinets stuffed with folders were left hanging open by whoever was in a mad dash for enlightenment on a client's case at a moments notice. Off to the side behind Ms. Jones custom made brown maple desk topped off with black marble stood a door with the nameplate, 'There is always a way, if the will is persistent.' Within this office was a smaller camouflaged room for business that needed to stay off the radar. Here is where William went after listening to my message. Coded messages, bug sweepers, untraceable phones, this world rivaled a spy wishing to remain unseen. My interest lay in William's ability to come by information that others found difficult to obtain.

The flight to the sunshine state was smooth except for my concern from not hearing what I needed to know to be able to proceed in the right direction once the plane touched down. Wine from a pretty stewardess pacified the stress with talk of getting together later for a dinner date. I couldn't help but feel like a man walking the last mile so I decided to let her be part of my last meal. Being new to the game of pursue and kill there were many things that escaped my notice that for a man like Damian I needed to be aware of if I was to survive long enough for justice to be served. Damian was well aware I'd be right behind him and was prepared. The cabby who picked me up found himself in a precarious situation when a car pulled up to his left with the passenger pointing a semi automatic at him motioning for him to stop. Oh shit escaped me in my moment of seeing my life flash before me a little prematurely.

"Tighten your seatbelt," the cabby said out of the side of his mouth as he looked at the gunman and nodded his head.

"What was that," My neck snapped back mercifully against the headrest. The Tachometer's needle fought to break out of it's casing as the cabbie slammed the clutch directly into fourth gear forcing eighteen inch steel belted tires to squeal out their intent at grabbing hold of the road which has now become a makeshift launching pad. In three seconds the twelve hundred plus horses under the engine shot the car into sixty mph hurtling us out of the line of fire and topping out at over a hundred in six seconds. When I was able to turn my head our friends were nowhere in sight.

"It seems there's more to you than meets the eye," I said when we were rolling at a respectable sixty mph.

"William got your message and said to sit tight until his Intel comes back with your request." The cabbie produced a Hotel reservation complete with dinner.

"What about those men who I'm pretty sure are still looking for me."

Three rugged heavy-duty trucks surrounded the armor plated black escalade, persuading it to be escorted to an area chosen for privacy. Four men at the pointed end of rocket grenades exited the vehicle with hands raised high. They were big men who loved their work, picked personally by Damian to do great harm to their targets before death. Eight men surrounded them as they were asked very politely to remove any and all weapons on their person.

Everyone but the four knew the deal, the only question was who and when. Two were chosen, two were handcuffed together to watch and wait. In this quiet place in the middle of a field far from the sounds of everyday living a ruling was to take place. A guilty verdict was already rendered at the time of capture but this is a civilized world so they are given a chance to redeem themselves. If one can walk away from his executioner, he is free to go, as is for all those lucky enough to follow after and not before. There was no bell, no referee, no rules and no pity.

The two men who were still handcuffed considered themselves lucky to be able to observe and familiarize themselves with the skills of their soon to be opponent. When he exited the truck they were more than confident a fight with him was in all probability never going to happen. They were all twice his size in every way possible. So sure were the two that had to fight first, that one stepped forward as he told his friend to relax, this was a done deal.

Without warning a flying kick to the solar plexus forced the wind out of the surprised man and he drops on all fours. As fast as he hits the ground he finds himself locked into what's called an arm bar, a wrestling move designed to immobilize or break bones. The grunts of pain are empathized by his partner who sees what he hears when the wrist, then shoulder and last to follow the elbow of the winded man are all fractured to the point of tearing through skin. A leg chop to the neck and in thirty seconds it was over. He now faces a very worried comrade. The gangster in a moment of cowardice copied the actions of those he had laughed at so many times before in their panicked attempt at escape. It did not work for them then and it would not work for him now but he tried anyway. From behind, death came by first taking out his feet. On the ground now, he pleads while being stomped into unconsciousness in a beating so horrific some of the men had to turn away.

Handcuffs are removed and the remaining two men are pushed toward their downed partners to try their luck. Their confidence is shaken in the two minutes it took for the sentence to be carried out. Their opponent still looks fresh and even scarier, hungry for more. There is a silent agreement between the two to fight together to ensure he stays off balance, so named double team to the death. They move on either side, both with experienced knowledge of the others capabilities solidifying their edge over an opponent they otherwise would have doubts about coming out of this unharmed. A sudden rush, one high one low, make him decide on how to handle the sudden moves of the two together. He drops low facing the man coming at him from high. His fist is a blur as it smashes into the groin of the first man then snaps back past him plowing his elbow into the bridge of the other man's face coming low. They are not together anymore, each suffering from a crippling shot stopping them in their tracks. These two are known to be torturers of women and children, part payment for a father, husband, or boyfriend not satisfying debts due to Damian. These two will live to see their bones broken one by painful one until something inside ceases to operate causing death.

"That situation is being handled," the cabbie said.

...A RIGHTEOUS END...

WITH THE PRECISION of trained commandos they stormed the warehouse overwhelming all inside without a single shot being fired but quite a few knockouts. In the basement below her eyes were shut tight, the pained grimace on her face obvious from biting her lips. It was a reflexive decision meant to trade off the focus from one reality to another. The huge hulk on top of her had just penetrated her most personal possession and made it his. She was one of five kidnapped women destined to serve as slaves to him first then the men, and finally to be sold on foreign soil never to be heard from again. An unplanned interruption at the end of a silent prayer was for this beautiful woman no less than a miracle. Tears, thank you's and a moment of revenge with a kick at the flaccid penis, which scant moments before, had speared itself deep into her virgin vaginal canal. Not satisfied, she coughed up a hunk of phlegm and scored a more direct hit upon Damian's face. Fifteen men surrounded him, guns trained to be sure there was not a chance in hell of an attempt to run. Whoever orchestrated this takeover wanted him alive, which in itself was a good sign. In this world, kill first ask questions later was the formula all gangsters abided by so his still being alive would seem like he's planned for other things.

It could be a rival who wants to expand his territory or an upstart like he was who thinks he has big enough cohones to take him on. It was obvious that a snitch within the organization set him up for his crew to have been taken over so easily. The snitch will be handled when the time comes but right now he'll tell this fool anything until he can regain the upper hand. After that an example will be made of all those involved, their friends and family members included.

Damian was led upstairs to see all his men tied up and all his pretty women standing there looking fresh as roses. The chance to break them in was past with only one of the flowers barely tasted. One thing's for sure, he admired the style in which his takedown transpired. He would be sure to upgrade security within his own organization once this mystery man is dead. Damian was transferred without delay out a back door and onto a van. He would never know that a deal was struck with some pissed relatives of past victims, the girls family members included, nor would he know that he wasn't the only one with a vast network of connections.

"Peacock, it's been years." Damian took a quick look around, unsure of whom this woman was referring to. He had been deposited into a shipping container cleaned and prepped for the occasion.

"You may not recall the young woman you fought that day outside the bar when you met my husband to be."

"I remember it wasn't a fight." He thought she looked familiar.

"I beg to differ but anyway, this is the man I think you want to see again." Pop entered the shipping container. It was an awkward meeting, a significant moment even for Damian who'd experienced just about everything life had to offer that interested him. The hows and the whys were not important now only what's next.

"Small world."

"That it is, Pop concurred."

"So I heard you had a contract out for us." Damian was puzzled as his mind sifted through years of hits with no recollection of these two. He didn't know them other than their random meeting those many years ago. He remembered it well, the months long hospital stay and the desire to repay him for the pain. At the time though, he was a rising star about to claim his empire by taking over territory once ran by Robert Hanson and company. The mysterious disappearances of him and five of his men had left the territory up for grabs. He had since spread his wings through three states and into the many neighborhoods that he seized control of.

"Are you Russell's parents," he asked in hopeful doubt."

"You hit the nail on the head," Mama answered.

"Well I'll be damned, if I had a known he was your kid, I'd a deaded all of you a long time ago."

"You still might have your wish." At least now once and for all he could see who was the best fighter of all time. Damian wondered as he did countless times through the years how the hell did this little man beat him. It would be a cathartic event nonetheless for all involved and a victory for who is left standing. He thought about the other kid who was tailing him and who should be very dead by now.

"Sweetheart, Rose eyed Damian as she addressed Pop, Peacock looks like he's anxious for round two." Damian removed his shirt to reveal six pack abs hard enough to withstand a hail of punches from the strongest of men and biceps strong enough to hold up a two hundred pound person on each arm.

"I'm not impressed, Rose said, let's get started." Rose took a couple of steps toward Damian right into a backhand that knocked her clear across the room. Pop moved on him so fast that the time for anyone to react had come and gone. He was in the middle of crushing Damian's windpipe when Rose beat him on the back to stop. Damian collapsed following the release of Pop's powerful grip, his only thought directed to labored breathing through a bruised windpipe. The swell on her face was already turning colors as Damian regained control of himself. That speed was a bitter reminder of their last meeting. Damian resolved he would fight much smarter than before.

Rose also received a bitter reminder of what Damian was capable of. She regressed back to her time of fighting with her best friend at her side. Chan made its debut out of retirement for the first time in a long time and with a flick of the wrist the six-inch blade was ready to draw blood.

"So the woman dies first," Damian acknowledged as he wrapped his shirt around his hand. Rose lunged at him with the knife leading the way but Damian with no fear of a woman wielding anything short of a .357 magnum was no match. He wanted to break her neck quickly so the real fight could start. He snatched her arm to bring her in close and with a quick spin she was facing Pop who was on pins and needles. His hands were in position to snap the fragile bone connection to her body when Rose plunged Chan into his thigh not once but three times forcing Damian to shove Rose as hard as he could away from him. Rose lost the blade as she fell across the small space and collided into the wall wincing at the sudden sharp pain in her shoulder as she struggled to get up before Damian reached her. He smashed a right into her side enjoying for a split second the feel of his rock hard fist plunging into her soft flesh. Rose screamed in pain as the next punch to the mid section lifted her up off the floor. It would have ended for Rose right there but Pop as always swooped her out of the way to the safety of his guards who stood ready for the word to kill Damian. They were all ushered out with specific instructions to make sure Rose gets taken care of.

"You want to punch some walls or something. It's unfair I get the chance to warm up on your pretty wife, but if you need more motivation, I'll let you in on a little secret. Your other son is dead by now thanks to me. Damian let out a howl while he waited for a reaction. Pop whose back was to the door reached behind and locked it.

-"A true gladiator to the end. Okay, let's see how much pain you can take." The big man came in close letting loose with a jab to the rib cage. Pop took the hit easy enough but knew he couldn't withstand too many more of the rock hard punches. Damian was ten years younger, still fighting and was a lot faster than Pop remembered. Damian's slight self-doubt was erased and he unleashed two more body blows knocking Pop down. He needed to finish him because he knew all to well that when you have the upper hand with this man you keep it. His attempt at stomping Pop was hindered with a catch and twist maneuver which sent him to the ground instead. Pop got up, more pissed than hurt at himself for letting Damian catch him.

...A FAMILY AFFAIR...

"YOU MIGHT WANT to unlock that door and run." Pop shook his head real slow. This time it was he that swung first backing Damian up to the wall with stinging punches. This is not going to end like before he thought, fight smart and find his weakness. He put up his fists as he circled trying to find a way to reach Pop. This time there was no pause, no breathers or allowances for getting your act together. They traded blows repeatedly, blood and sweat finding places to settle all over the small container that for this period in time is an arena. Damian used all his skills as he tried to find a way to weaken Pop enough to deliver a blow to cripple his capabilities so he could end this and figure a way out. Pop had his own plans and staying close to the giant lessened his power at such a short distance and like a woodpecker tapping repeatedly at the same spot on a tree, so did Pop hammer the same spot on Damian's shoulder until it became apparent he could do no more than swing it around weakly. Fifteen minutes have gone by and they are exhausted but giving up is a death sentence so they fight. With his good right arm he attempts to grab hold of any body part to gain a few seconds rest but receives a jaw jarring punch sending him to face the ground. He glances briefly at the locked door then at Pop who is shakes his head again. From the floor Damian threw a Hail Mary punch at the looming figure of Pop over him on the off chance that he was lucky enough to score a knockout. It's brushed aside, he is picked up and thrown down so Pop can to go to work on that six-pack he redeveloped over the years and was so proud of.

A knock on the door paused the onslaught together with a welcome sigh of relief from Damian. The makeshift arena is now crowded with Pop's guards,

Mama and myself. The scene that confronts us looks like something out of a horror movie. Their busted up and bleeding bodies were a testament to the vicious battle that was taking place unseen until now. Blood splatter dotted the walls and floor with most of it concentrated on the two combatants who were before us. It appeared if we hadn't come in just then, Damian would be dead now. I was thankful he wasn't. I lived for this moment and there was no way I would be denied. He hit my mother, me knowing only because I was informed on my arrival, and my father stood before me bloody and hurt. Pop was too old for this and I was in the best shape of my life even though this was the biggest man I'd ever seen.

"So this is the man that has caused me so much grief? There could be but one answer but I'm a man that needs to hear it. Mama said yes.

-Is he dead?" Pop said not yet. Relax Pop I don't want you fighting my battles." I began removing my shirt.

"Put your shirt back on son, this man is a professional street fighter and you are no match for him. Your Momma almost got killed because she felt the need to fight him." I cut Pop off, declaring I was not my mother.

"Peacock's half dead Pop, let the boy have a go," Mama said. The name Peacock rung a bell but didn't register right away.

"Yea, let your punk ass kid have a go." His request was answered by my immediate attack on him. Damian's left arm could barely move but he was more than capable with his right arm. Without so much as a second thought he knocked me across the small area, followed my motion and was on me before I hit the wall. That big right arm with the huge fist attached to it wavered over my face unable to complete its mission. Behind him was Pop holding it firm with his arms locked around his neck and shoulder. Realizing my own foolishness, I moved out of the way and let my father finish what he started. Thrown up against a wall, Damian had a flashback of the first ass kicking he received from Pop and instinctively knew this was going to be far worse and Pop made sure his instincts were correct. He talked real low maybe an inch from Damian's right ear. It was a voice devoid of any emotion yet the chill from the tone went right through me.

"We gonna do this until you beg for me to take your life," He said. I could say the first few punches were the worse and Pop got tired as the beating went on but then I'd be lying. His bulging veins pulsated through thick battle scarred muscles as the jackhammer action of his arms caved in Damian's rock hard abs turning them into a mass of mushy searing pain. Watching Damian being beat to death wasn't for the weak but we couldn't turn away. Mesmerized, all of us stood quiet while Pop, sweat dripping, spit foaming, nose running a mix of blood and snot put in work on Damian for one hour straight, rest, revive him and pounded some more this time mixing it up a bit. At some point my eyes closed but the grunts from Pop after every powerful blow then the sound of a forced groan from Damian on the receiving end maintained a vivid picture in my mind. By the second hour Damian begged for Pop to please take his life. When it was over we walked out of there as a family intact.

...EPILOGUE...

AT DINNER LATER that evening all my questions were answered. First, Russell had informed Mama about everything, the contract on the family, the role Mink played and all about Damian. The whole fake sickness and death was because it was unknown how extensive Damian's network of eyes watching were so everything had to be realistic. When asked why they didn't include me in any of their plans, I got the side eye from both parents. It seems they concluded, I hadn't been in my right mind since the arrest which although understandable would only compound the problem with my involvement. They surmised one rash decision by myself would put me in either prison or the grave and Damian nor Mink was worth that consequence. Crazy ass Mink they figured could wait on their return trip while Damian who was the real threat get taken care of since I was the only one in line for the hit whose deadline was close. They even knew that at the last minute Damian wanted Mink to take me out which is the reason why Pop made the fake phone call about the feds closing in. They knew Damian would head to Florida, his main headquarters first before taking a long vacation out of the country. William was supposed to alert me to Damian's whereabouts knowing I would follow immediately removing me out of Mink's crosshairs. I almost screwed up everything by killing and blowing her up surprising the hell out of all concerned. It took William's special services to clear the mess I left at Mink's.

"See, unstable," Mama reiterated. After the close call at the airport, William made sure I stayed far away from all the action until he got a call from Mama.

One thing was for certain, after meeting the giant Mama called Peacock from all those years ago an apology was in order. In my mind, she exaggerated a little about Pop's abilities and the viciousness of the two when they met. I have a new found respect for Pop's skills and am glad he was on my side. Mama raised her glass,

"Toast to putting another storm behind us."

"Yes, yes, I'll toast to that!"

THE END

Kenneth N. Johnson is a native New Yorker, born in the South Bronx and now residing in Queens. This is his first published work of fiction with more to follow.